Every Month Original
Novels, Stories, and Articles

MONTHLY

USA Today Bestselling Writer
Dean Wesley Smith

I0554016

TABLE OF CONTENTS

SHORT STORIES

Not Salable for Sale
   A Poker Boy Story   6

*The Life and Death
of Fortune Cookie Tyrant*   16

A Time to Dream
   A Captain Brian Saber Story   48

Tumbling Down the Nighttime   58

In Search of the Perfect Orgasm   70

FULL NOVEL

Star Rain
   A Seeders Universe Novel   76

SERIAL BOOK

Writing into the Dark
               Part 1 of 2   28

NONFICTION

Introduction:
   A Writing Book   3

SMITH'S MONTHLY ISSUE #26

Introduction
A WRITING BOOK

Something kind of different and fun in this issue.

Instead of serializing a novel, I'm going to serialize a nonfiction book, sort of how I did the golf book earlier in this magazine. But this is a writing book and will only be in this issue and the next.

The writing book is called *Writing into the Dark.*

My blog, for those of you who follow it, tends to be mostly about writing in various ways, although I do post collection pictures at times and cat pictures as well.

But mostly my blog talks about the life of a professional writer.

A few years back I did a lecture and a series of blogs on how to write a novel without an outline. That's basically what "writing into the dark" means.

Writing into the Dark has sold well and has gotten a lot of positive responses.

So figured it would be fun to have it here just for two issues.

Then in issue #28, a novel serial will start. Finally, after thirty years, I am bringing my first published novel back into print and serializing it here.

So stay tuned for that.

In this issue I also have three special short stories out of the past.

All three were published in anthologies and I have had them for sale in electronic standalone for a few years now. But thought this issue would be a good one to put them together.

Two are set in nursing homes. One is the origin story, the very first Captain Brian Saber story I ever wrote. Another is a story that sort of predated my Nebula Award-nominated story "In the Shade of the Slowboat Man." This story is called "Tumbling Down the Nighttime."

The third fun story is called "In Search of the Perfect Orgasm or How Doing it with a Big Lizard Can Be Fun."

Thanks for the Support

Dean Wesley Smith

Yes, that's the title, almost longer than the story.

I do a full introduction to the short story about some various things that happened with that story. The story behind the story, so-to-speak.

The novel in this issue is *Star Rain: A Seeders Universe Novel.*

Star Rain followed right where *Star Mist* left off last issue. The Seeders Universe just keeps getting bigger and bigger.

Plus this issue leads off with a Poker Boy story, as normal.

So I hope you enjoy the five stories and the novel and the first half of one of my writing books.

—Dean Wesley Smith
November 23rd, 2015

With more than a hundred published novels and more than seventeen million copies of his books in print, USA Today bestselling author Dean Wesley Smith knows how to outline. And he knows how to write a novel without an outline.

In this WMG Writer's Guide, Dean takes you step-by-step through the process of writing without an outline and explains why not having an outline boosts your creative voice and keeps you more interested in your writing.

Want to enjoy your writing more and entertain yourself? Then toss away your outline and Write into the Dark.

Coming Next Issue in Smith's Monthly

GRAPEVINE SPRINGS
A Thunder Mountain Novel

Lenny the Leprechaun's wife went missing and now he wants Poker Boy to find her. Not known for finding people, Poker Boy only rescues people and dogs and the world in the process.

Mrs. Lenny's vanishing act seems to have no connection to Poker Boy. Until Poker Boy looks deeper.

Then Poker Boy knows he might be able to save her, if she still lives. Which he doubts.

NOT SALABLE FOR SALE
A Poker Boy Story

ONE

SEEING A LEPRECHAUN appear in a small casino in the mountains of Oregon can make even a professional poker player like me lose my train of thought.

I flipped my A-10 off-suit into the muck and turned to my right as the leprechaun waved at me.

He had on the standard, leprechaun-green top hat that didn't cover his pointed ears but sort of rode on them like they were training wheels for the big hat. He had a green jacket, brown pants, and a long-stemmed pipe in his mouth that didn't seem to be lit. It stuck out of his scraggly red beard like a weed out of a ragged lawn.

He wasn't any taller than the back of a poker chair, and was as skinny as a flagpole. Somehow he climbed onto a chair, on top of an empty poker table, and then sat down, his big brown shoes with gold buckles dangling over the edge of the table like he was a kid sitting in a huge chair.

I glanced around to see if anyone else had noticed the new visitor.

No one had, even though there were three tables of eight going at the moment. Spirit Winds Casino in the Oregon mountains didn't have many people in the poker room at midnight on a Wednesday.

I was here because I was just waiting for my girlfriend to get off work at the MGM Grand Casino in Las Vegas, and I figured the plucking of tourists would be easier here tonight than in Vegas. And since, as Poker Boy, I could jump back and forth instantly with my Jump Anywhere Power, it didn't matter where I played.

Besides, this was my old home casino; I knew everyone here, and it was comfortable. There was a lot to be said about comfort.

Now a stupid leprechaun had interrupted my nice evening.

I had only seen leprechauns in Vegas at the Okey-Doke Casino out on the old highway. It was one of those places hidden with magic, so that no one knew it was there unless you were taken there. I had helped solve a big problem there a while back, so maybe this guy was just coming to say hi and thank me again.

I doubted it. I had learned that no one could ever trust a leprechaun. And I had no plan on trusting this one, either.

I pushed away from the table and tossed the dealer a ten-dollar chip. "If I'm not back in thirty minutes, rack them and hold them for me, would you?"

The dealer nodded and rapped the chip on the felt in acknowledgement.

I adjusted my black leather coat and zipped it up, then made sure my black fedora-like hat was on solid before turning away from the table.

Already the little skinny guy had cost me money. My hunch was it was only going to go downhill from here.

"Where'd you leave the pot of gold?" I asked as I walked past him.

"Funny," he said, his voice deep and raspy and not fitting his thin, small body at all. "Very damn funny."

Leprechauns hated being teased about their pots of gold. They had lost all of it, every damn pot, a couple of centuries before in a bad bet with a few aliens who happened to be visiting Earth at the time. It was still a touchy subject.

I just kept walking, letting him jump down from the table and follow me. I had no intention of carrying on a conversation with an invisible man while on casino security cameras. That wouldn't do my reputation any good at all.

Besides, I needed a break and some fresh air.

At a fast walk, I weaved my way through the slot machines, cutting through all the smoke and older people plugging the machines like the world was about to end and they wanted to get rid of every dollar before it did.

As we neared the front door of the casino, the little guy finally caught up with me, his pipe in one hand, his other hand holding his hat onto his head as he ran. He was panting and swearing lightly under his breath.

"Shouldn't smoke so much," I said as I pushed open the door and hesitated to let him go through ahead of me.

"You shouldn't be such a jerk," the little guy said in his deep voice. He sounded more like a country-western singer and he didn't have any accent at all.

"You're the one who is bothering me," I said, heading out toward the parking lot to where I knew there was a small dead spot in the security cameras. The fall night air felt great after wading through the smoke around those slot machines. Clean and pure.

I glanced at my watch. Still over two hours before I had to pick up Patty at the MGM Grand.

Patty was also called Front Desk Girl, and she was a superhero in the hospitality part of the gambling universe. We fit together perfectly and made a great team. She had long brown hair and wonderful brown eyes I loved getting lost in. She was only a few inches shorter than I was, but when she wore heels we seemed to be the same size.

"I just came to ask for help from the great Poker Boy," the leprechaun said.

"Sarcasm just won't get me doing anything," I said. "So what's your name?"

He glared at me. I knew that knowing any magical creature's name gave me power over them. And he knew I knew it. He had no intention of giving me that kind of power.

"So what do I call you?" I asked.

"Lenny," he said. He clearly must have already figured that's the name he would use with me.

"Lenny the Leprechaun," I said, shaking my head as I reached the dead area in the security cameras and stopped, sitting down on the edge of a planter to be more at his level. "Got it."

"I'm an elf," he said, getting red in the face and spreading his thin legs into a fighting stance in front of me. Old elves who wore green and smoked pipes for some reason never liked to be called leprechauns. No one had explained that to me yet. Someday I would ask Stan, the God of Poker, why that was.

"Sorry," I said. "So what can I do for you?"

Lenny took the pipe out of his mouth and stuck it in his belt, then adjusted his tall hat and then his green vest. Then he went to pacing in front of me, two steps, turn, two steps. With his short legs he didn't go far in either direction.

He clearly didn't want to tell me why he had come to find me.

I clicked on my Trust Me super power," added a little Calming Power and aimed it at him.

He suddenly stopped pacing and faced me.

"Nice magic," he said, taking a deep breath and clearly relaxing. "Thanks, I feel better."

I had never thought of my powers as magic before, but I suppose they were. And I had never tried them on a magical creature before now. Learn something every day, even from a Leprechaun.

"You're welcome," I said, switching off my power. "Now, what's happening?"

"Mrs. Lenny, my wife, is missing."

TWO

NOW, OF ALL the things a leprechaun might come to me for help with, I sure would have never thought it would be to find his wife. I didn't even know where leprechauns lived. I had heard that the ones around Vegas lived in magically hidden forests and glens in valleys up by Lake Mead. But I would have to ask someone above me in the ranks if even that was right.

And besides, I was a superhero in the world of gambling, specializing in poker, thus the name, Poker Boy. I wasn't Missing-Persons-Boy, although I wouldn't be surprised that a superhero with that name actually existed. Gods and superheroes seemed to exist for just about everything on the planet.

So he had to have a special reason for coming to me.

"I'm sorry to hear about your wife," I said, actually being sincere. "But not sure what you think I can do to help."

"I was told you would be the best person to help me," he said, looking very worried.

"Who told you that?" More than likely this was just a joke being played on me, and so far I had fallen for it and taken the little guy a little too seriously.

"The general manager of the Okey-Doke Casino checked around and found out you were the best. He asked your boss if it would be all right if I contacted you, and he said sure."

"My boss?" I asked, now stunned. "Who do you think my boss is?"

The little guy sort of shrugged. "Some guy named Stan I think."

That was enough. I looked up into the air and shouted "Stan!"

An instant later Stan, the God of Poker, appeared beside me in the parking lot. He had on his normal brown slacks, short-sleeved business shirt that matched his slacks and loafers. He had nothing at all distinctive about his face and his brown hair was cut short, but not too short. Perfect camouflage for a poker player. He could walk down the street and no one would notice him.

Stan glanced around and nodded. "Dead camera area, huh?"

"And fresh air," I said.

"A little chilly," he said and a brown sweater appeared on him.

"You know Lenny here," I said, indicating the leprechaun.

Stan nodded. "Never met, but heard of the problem. Sorry to hear about your wife. If anyone can help you, it's Poker Boy."

Okay, so now I was convinced that Stan was in on this joke as well. Gods were well known for pulling pranks and practical jokes. And Stan had done his share over the years.

I stood, adjusting my leather coat. "Okay, so tell me the punch line so I can get back to my game."

Lenny the Leprechaun looked pained and Stan just looked puzzled. After a moment Stan seemed to catch on to what I was saying, and he shook his head and looked at Lenny.

"You haven't told him your problem yet?"

"I told him my wife was missing," he said, defensively.

"But you didn't tell him where, did you?" Stan asked, staring down at the little elf.

Lenny looked almost insulted. "Where else would my wife go missing that I couldn't find her?"

I shook my head and started away from the dead area of the casino parking lot. "I've got a game to finish."

"Silicon Suckers," Stan said.

The two words stopped me cold and I turned around and went back.

Silicon Suckers are a very, very old race of beings that have been on Earth far longer than humans. They are often mistaken for the "Grays" by alien-watchers. The Silicon Suckers live in what they call "castles" under desert areas. They have huge, city-sized caverns and hundreds of miles of tunnels under the desert outside of Vegas on the north side of town. The Silicon Suckers control a large amount of desert all around Las Vegas. I have done numbers of favors for them over the years, so I am an honored guest in their cities.

They also killed an old girlfriend of mine when she wouldn't return some sacred silicon a doctor had put into her breasts. I had warned her many times that the Silicon Suckers would get their silicon back one way or another. And they did.

I ignored Lenny and looked at Stan. "I thought the fairy world and the Silicon Suckers were not on speaking terms."

"They aren't," Stan said, clearly disgusted. "But Mrs. Lenny thought she might be able to negotiate with them for a small piece of property near the lake."

"Did she ask anyone why that property would never be for sale?" I asked, stunned. The only property the Silicon Suckers controlled near Lake Mead was a cliff face that represented some of their deepest beliefs and history. I was told that the cliff was the last remaining wall of their most ancient city.

"I doubt it," Stan said. "Otherwise she wouldn't be missing."

"We thought it would be a good addition to a charming pool under the wall," Lenny said. "Make some slides on it, diving platforms, you know the drill."

I just shook my head in disgust. Stan just smiled. His poker face was better than mine.

If Lenny's wife had tried to even make an offer on that cliff face, she was long since dead. Just the offer would be so insulting to the Silicon Suckers that Lenny's wife would be moisture for their underground gardens.

I was about to tell Lenny that, when it dawned on me that I knew exactly where Lenny's wife was, and that she hadn't even gotten to insulting the Silicon Suckers by telling them her people wanted to make a recreational area out of a scared place.

I started laughing and both Stan and Lenny looked at me like I had gone crazy.

"Where did she try to go in?" I asked Lenny between laughs.

"At the large Downtown Vegas billboard off the highway on the north," Lenny said, staring at me. "And what's so damned funny about my wife being missing?"

"She's not dead, that's what," I said. "She is a magical being, right?"

"Of course," Lenny said, clearly angry, his little frame shaking.

Then Stan started laughing as well. He understood enough about the Silicon Suckers to know that they must know a person's true name before they will be allowed inside of their castles. And magical people won't give out their real names unless really pressed, thus she would never be allowed into any Silicon Sucker city.

"I'll go get her," I said to Stan. "Take Lenny here back to Vegas and wait for my shout."

THREE

STAN NODDED and I jumped to a small café on a side street in downtown Vegas. "The Diner" was my team's favorite hangout, and it had the best hamburgers and milkshakes in town. It was decorated like one of the old 1960s diners, and was run by Madge, a superhero in the food service world.

When I appeared, Madge was behind the counter and there were no other customers in the place. Madge had her hair up like normal in a tight bun, and her brown waitress dress was two sizes too small as was always normal as well.

She turned around and smiled. "I was expecting you, Poker Boy," she said. "I heard that little leprechaun fellow was going to ask you to help rescue his wife from the Silicon Suckers."

"Word travels fast," I said, smiling as she placed three thermoses of hot chocolate on the counter in front of me.

She knew that hot chocolate was the drug of choice for Silicon Suckers. It was more precious to them than gold was to humans. I had watched one Silicon Sucker take just a drop of hot chocolate and go into orgasmic shudders.

Three thermoses full would give me some real bargaining power for Mrs. Lenny.

"Thanks, Madge," I said, dropping a hundred dollar bill on the counter. "Does that cover everything?"

She smiled and picked up the bill. "More than enough."

Now I was down a hundred and ten for this adventure.

"See you soon," I said.

I put one thermos into each pocket of my leather coat and then held the other one and jumped to the billboard on the highway.

The lights of the billboard lit up the surrounding highway, and a moment after I arrived on the sand under the billboard a car sped past, headed out of town. The driver must have gotten a shock, me appearing in front of him like that.

The air was cold and the wind light, but brisk. I was glad I had on my coat. The high-desert winter cold wasn't far away.

I moved over to where I knew the entrance of the Silicon Sucker's city was, in the side of a sand hillside about twenty feet from the billboard.

A huge pair of high-heeled shoes lay there in the sand. And when I say huge, I don't mean size twelve. Those things would be considered small boats for some people and I had no doubt that Lenny could put both feet into one shoe and have room to move his toes around. If leprechauns even had toes.

I didn't see any tiny leprechaun shoes nearby, so I moved to the entrance, kicked off my own tennis shoes, and then bowed at the empty night air.

"Poker Boy would request the honor of entering a sacred city of the honorable Silicon Suckers. I have brought a gift."

I bowed slightly and held up the thermos of hot chocolate.

A second later the opening to the Silicon Sucker underground city appeared and I stepped inside.

I was met ten steps inside by two Silicon Suckers. They bowed and wished me long life and a pleasant visit to their city.

I handed over my thermos of hot chocolate and the two carried it away carefully, both holding it like it was a bomb and might explode.

A moment later another Silicon Sucker appeared and bowed to me slightly. "It is a pleasure to see you again, Poker Boy."

"The pleasure is mine," I said, bowing as well. All Silicon Suckers looked pretty much the same, so I had no idea if I had met this one before or not.

He turned and I followed him through the narrow tunnel to a larger tunnel where a very, very large woman knelt on the sand floor looking very, very tired. At least she had not yet committed the deadly sin of falling asleep or leaning against a wall. She knew that much it seemed about Silicon Sucker rules.

Even kneeling and slumping, she was taller than I was, and I could barely fit in these tunnels. She must have walked on her knees just to get this far.

She was wearing a brown dress that looked dusty, and her hair was curly brown and short against her head. She had a very wide face with a nose that seemed to spread from one cheek to the other. At one point she had had on makeup, but that had run with tears.

I was almost afraid to ask, but I did anyway. "Is your husband a leprechaun?"

She looked over at me, startled, clearly seeing me for the first time. Then she smiled. "He is."

I turned to my host and spoke in Silicon Sucker native. "I have come to bargain for this being's release from your wonderful city. Her husband has need of her at home."

"She will not tell us her name," my host said.

I had no doubt they had not even asked, but had just expected it.

"It is against her culture," I said.

"Then we cannot release her."

I knew better at that moment to insult him by trying to bribe him with the hot chocolate in my coat.

"If she tells you her real name, will she be allowed to leave your fine city?"

"We will consider it," my host said.

I turned to Mrs. Lenny who was looking at me with horror since I had spoken to the Silicon Sucker in his own language of strange ticks and snorts and hisses.

"If you tell this one Silicon Sucker your real name, you may be able to leave."

She started to object, but I held up my hand for her to stop.

"I will cover my ears to make sure I have not heard your name. I know doing so is against your beliefs, but if you want to live, you now have no choice. I will never mention to anyone you have done so."

She again started to speak but again I stopped her with a raised hand.

"If you complain, I may not be able to get you out of here at all. Say nothing to this Silicon Sucker but 'My name is… I am honored in your presence.'"

She nodded.

"And do not lie. It must be your full name. They will know if it is not. Nod only if you understand."

She nodded again.

"I will cover my ears now, you will state your full and real name. Then I will bargain for your release."

I could tell she was so tired, she didn't care anymore. I knew she was violating something that was important, but at this point she just had no choice if she wanted to see little Lenny again.

I covered my ears and after a moment I could see her speaking.

When she stopped the Silicon Sucker bowed to her and I knew her name had been a true one.

I turned to my host. "I have a gift for my host in exchange for the release of this being."

I removed another thermos of hot chocolate.

"Is her life worth such a price?" he asked.

"It is," I said. "And for allowing me to speak on her behalf, I have another gift for my wonderful friends."

I pulled out the other thermos of hot chocolate.

I thought my host might actually gasp. But somehow he maintained his poise and nodded. "Your friend may leave with you, Poker Boy."

"Thank you," I said, bowing.

"And you are always a welcomed, honored guest in our castles."

At that moment two other Silicon Suckers appeared and took the two thermoses from me, then the three of them walked away.

I held up my hand that Mrs. Lenny should not speak, then indicated that she should follow me back toward the entrance.

She did, somehow walking on her knees without touching either the walls or the floor with her hands. I had no doubt those sand burns on her knees were going to take some time to heal.

When we got outside, the entrance behind us vanished and she fell panting into the sand.

"Stan!" I said into the air.

Stan and Lenny the Leprechaun appeared. Lenny rushed to the huge woman and tried to hug her. He managed to sort of hug one arm.

Then he tried to help her to her feet and somehow managed to not get crushed.

Standing up in bare feet, Mrs. Lenny the Leprechaun stood a good twelve feet tall. She could change the light bulbs on the billboard without a ladder if she wanted to.

She rested her hand gently on her husband's shoulder while he sort of hugged her thigh.

"Thank you," she said in a very high, faint voice.

"Yes, thank you," Lenny said in a very low voice, nodding to me. "They were right about you, Poker Boy."

"Let's go home," Mrs. Lenny said, indicating that Lenny should pick up her shoes.

"Anything you say, my little sweetness," Lenny said and he managed to heft both shoes and they vanished.

I looked at Stan, shocked.

And he looked back at me, clearly just as shocked.

"You didn't tell me Mrs. Lenny Leprechaun was a giant," I said.

"I didn't know," Stan said, shaking his head.

Then, before we both broke down laughing right there outside of the Silicon Suckers castle, I picked up my shoes and said, "Meet you after two at The Diner?"

He nodded about to break down in laughter and I jumped back to the parking lot of my favorite casino in Oregon.

I laughed all the way inside trying to keep my imagination from running wild and failing miserably.

I collected my chips that had been racked for me. I was just over a hundred up for the night, so I ended up only slightly behind for the evening with all the rescue expenses.

When I jumped to pick up Patty at the MGM Grand in Vegas, I gave her a hug. She fit perfectly in my arms and I started laughing again thinking of Lenny hugging his wife's thigh.

"What's so funny?" Patty asked looking up at me with those wonderful brown eyes of hers.

"I just like the way we fit together is all," I said.

"So do I," she said, giving me a hug. "Are you propositioning a very tired woman?"

Suddenly the image of Lenny and his wife in bed together went through my mind and I shuddered.

A really bad reaction to what Patty had asked.

Really bad.

And it took me and Stan both to the end of hamburgers and milkshakes at The Diner to explain.

~

Now Available
from all your favorite booksellers
in trade paper and electronic editions.

Dean Wesley Smith

USA Today Bestselling Writer

Sometimes
the best cookie
brings more than
just a fortune...

THE LIFE AND DEATH OF FORTUNE COOKIE TYRANT

When destined to rule the world, you must always be cautious when looking for more power.

Steven, soon be known as Fortune Cookie Tyrant, hoped to find even more power and fortune by looking in the same place he first found his luck, fortune, and ability to rule.

But sometimes the best cookie brings more than just a fortune.

THE LIFE AND DEATH OF FORTUNE COOKIE TYRANT

ONE

You will live your life by direct instructions.
—Chinese Fortune Cookie

THE ORIGIN of a tyrant is often a mixture of common sense, wild strangeness, and a lot of luck. Those three factors led to the creation of one of the world's most feared and misunderstood dictators, Fortune Cookie Tyrant, or just FC among his minions when speaking of him in private.

Every great ruler's story usually starts with a single event. Seven-month-old Fortune Cookie Tyrant, then named Steven, had just soiled his diaper while strapped into his high-chair near his mother, Betty, at the end of the table at Fon Wong's Emporium and Lounge. The smell of Steven's little event mixed well with the smell of the last few bites of fried rice and over-cooked chow mein, so, for a while, no one noticed.

Steven's dad, Frank, burped, pushed his plate aside and leaned back, patting his growing beer gut. "Good food."

Every Wednesday night he said the same thing after eating the same dinner at Fon Wong's, so Betty just nodded and kept eating. He always finished ahead of her and then wanted to leave, so her only hope now of enjoying the last few bites of food was to work fast.

Steven, being somewhat uncomfortable with the nature call, started to "fuss," as his mother called it.

Sensing that Steven was going to be a problem, and wanting to just finish the last few mouthfuls of her dinner, Betty reached over and gave Steven a fortune cookie that had been left on top of the bill. It had been her cookie, but at this point it didn't matter.

Distracted for the moment from the loaded diaper, Steven played with the cookie, finally managing to crack it open before putting it in his mouth, fortune and all.

"Whoa there, big fella," his dad said, reaching over and pulling the paper and most of the cookie from Steven's mouth. "You gotta read the fortune before eating it."

Betty laughed and just kept eating, glad for the few extra moments, as Frank opened the fortune and read it aloud. "Big fella, it says you will live your life by direct instructions."

Steven's father grunted and glanced at Betty before tossing the slip of paper on the table between the dirty plates. "What kinda stupid fortune is that?"

Actually, unknown to either Frank or Betty or the growingly more uncomfortable Fortune Cookie Tyrant, it was a charmed fortune, cursed by the magic of an angry Chinese man whose brother had slept with his wife.

The cookie had been specially made for the man's brother, with the curse on the fortune intended to let the angry man push his brother around and pay him back for his deed by giving him fortune cookies with really nasty instructions inside. But as luck would have it, the charmed cookie that was to set the entire process in motion was lost in the packing process. Instead of being sent to the angry man who could then give it to his brother, it was added to a shipment headed for the United States, where it ended up in Steven's hands at Fon Wong's Emporium and Lounge.

Common sense, wild luck, and a strange curse had come together to change Steven into Fortune Cookie Tyrant, a man whose entire life and the future of the entire world was to be steered by the fortunes included in small desserts.

As life would have it, Steven's parents were killed the following weekend in a tragic deer hunting accident. Steven was sent to live with his wicked and uncaring aunt who hated Chinese food. Thus it was twenty years and five months before Steven got his next "fortune" and came to realize his true powers for evil.

TWO

THE DATE with Amy wasn't going well.

They had met in a freshman United States history class at the university and smiled at each other for a few classes before Steven had had the courage to talk to her, and eventually ask her for a date. Steven, at this point in his life, was not an attractive man. He looked like a bad cross between a movie nerd scientist and Ichabod Crane. He had just come into his last growth and had the social skills of a stumbling tenth grader, even though he was in college.

Amy was no real catch, either, but for Steven, any woman who agreed to go out with him was someone special. He had fantasized for days about making love to her.

Now, sitting in Amy's favorite Chinese restaurant, the conversation had lagged and become strained toward the end of dinner, and all Steven could think about was how he was going to get her back to his dorm room and into bed. He had no idea what she was thinking about, and had no idea how to ask her. In fact, he had no idea at all what to even talk about next. It was that sort of uncomfortable moment.

She picked up the tray holding the two fortune cookies, smiled at him from behind her thick glasses, and said, "You first."

He took the small cookie, she handed him the tray, then she took the second. He was about to pop the entire thing into his mouth when she broke hers open and took out the little slip of paper.

He did the same, puzzling at the strange feeling that came over him when he read the words, "Intuition will help you solve puzzling problems."

He glanced up at her as she shook her head at her fortune and then flipped it toward him. "Dumb, really dumb. I'm supposed to come into money shortly. Yeah, that's going to happen. Why can't they ever do anything original with these cookies?"

Steven wasn't listening. He knew instantly how to solve his problem, how to get her back to his dorm room, and into a position they might both enjoy. He didn't know how he knew, but with one look at her, he just knew.

Not allowing himself to stop and think about what he was doing, he reached his hand past the half-eaten plate of pork rice and touched her hand, looking into her startled eyes.

"I've got a confession to make," he said, letting himself smile just a little to not make his words seem threatening, "I've been sitting here this entire dinner trying not to stare at you. You're the most beautiful woman I have ever seen, and I just had to tell you that."

His words were smooth, smoother than he had ever spoken in his life, his voice deeper, his tone perfect, his eyes focused and caring. Steven marveled at himself as this new power took over his body, smoothly talking to Amy, making her laugh, making her squeeze his hand with the promise of the night.

From that moment on, he said the exact right thing at every exact right moment.

And considering that he had never been with a woman his entire life, and had only watched a few porn films, he was a perfect lover as well. It seemed that the power to know how to solve her needs, as well as his own, stuck with him long after the dinner was gone.

The next morning, after she had left with a long kiss and a hope for more time with him, the power didn't go with her. He just sort of knew how to solve problems, how to deal with things that just the day before would have left him puzzled and lost.

And from that day forward his classes, once challenging, got insanely easy. He knew how to get extra money when he needed it, how to make himself look better, and how to talk a woman into bed. Within a few months, he had a new wardrobe, had moved into an apartment, had bought a nice car, and still had a perfect grade point average.

Fortune Cookie Tyrant had taken his first step toward world domination and control, and not once did he link it to the fortune in the cookie, thus it was over a year before he took his second step toward his true destiny.

THREE

THE FOOTBALL GAME had been awful, and the team had lost badly, making Steven's mood at the Chinese dinner more somber than excited. He had never played football because he had always been too skinny and uncoordinated and his aunt had hated the game. But that didn't matter. He loved watching football, and over the last year had become one of the university team's biggest fans.

Across the table from Steven was his date, Jane, a woman with few brains, long legs, and a sexual appetite that needed to be fed often. At first the combination had attracted him, along with the fact that she was way out of his class on looks. But now, after dating for almost three weeks, he had to admit she was starting to wear him out.

Besides that, the conversation with her when they weren't making love was deadly dull.

"Oh, I love fortune cookies," Jane said, clapping her hands like she was a kid and reaching for one as the waiter set the bill down on the table.

Steven just shook his head, took the leftover cookie and broke it apart. Then he read the fortune. "Your natural ability with words will make you a leader that many will follow."

"Yeah, right," he said, flipping the fortune back onto the table. But he could feel that something around the table, around the entire restaurant had suddenly changed. Everyone was looking at him. It creeped him out.

He checked to make sure he didn't have a big hunk of pork hanging off his nose or a noodle caught in his hair. Nothing. Even his zipper was up and tight.

"What shall we do next?" Jane asked, her eyes peering into his like his every word suddenly mattered. She was leaning forward, showing him a nice view of one of her best assets.

Steven glanced around at everyone watching him as the silence in the restaurant settled in.

Creepy.

He glanced back down at the table and the fortune caught his eye. "... a leader that many will follow." His intuition sense told him that he had gained something special tonight.

But for the first time in a long time, he wanted to test that sense.

He looked directly at Jane. He'd had a great dream the other night about watching her dance naked. Why not try that. "I'm up for some dancing naked in the street."

He said it just loud enough for most of the patrons in the small restaurant to hear. He wanted to just shock those staring at him, make them look away. But actually, more than anything, he wanted to see Jane dancing naked in the street. That would be a lot of fun.

"Great idea!" Jane said, again clapping her hands together like she was ten. "I wish I had thought of that. I'm ready when you are."

He swallowed and glanced at the slip of paper on the table, then up at Jane.

Now Available
from all your favorite booksellers
in trade paper and electronic editions.

USA TODAY BESTSELLING AUTHOR

DEAN WESLEY

SMITH

THE HIGH EDGE

A SEEDERS UNIVERSE NOVEL

Maybe this fantasy was about to come true.

Then he noticed that instead of snickers from the other patrons around the restaurant, they were nodding, laughing, putting their napkins on unfinished meals, talking to each other about how wonderful it would be to dance naked in the street.

Steven sat there, stunned. The entire restaurant was getting ready to follow him out the front door.

He picked up the little piece of paper with the fortune, stared at it, one word coming clearly to focus. "...many..."

Which meant not all. He glanced around at all the excited people getting ready to follow him.

There were two people out of the thirty or so who weren't getting ready to do anything. They were just sitting, looking stunned at what was being suggested around them. One was a young woman with long black hair, and the other a blond-headed jock-like man with a chiseled jaw.

Not everyone would follow his lead.

But most would.

A good lesson to learn.

He shrugged. He had to see where this would lead, but his intuition power told him that it would lead anywhere he wanted it to lead.

Ten minutes later, fully clothed, he stood on the sidewalk watching as the entire customer base of the restaurant except for two, danced naked in the street. Cars had stopped and many onlookers in the buildings were staring. Luckily, it wasn't a bad sight, considering it was a restaurant full of college students. Steven told Jane, loud enough for everyone close by to hear, to keep dancing and that he would be back.

Jane nodded and everyone kept dancing to some silent music, all stark nude. With his words, a number of pedestrians and drivers who had been watching nodded, took their clothes off and joined in.

The two that hadn't followed him were standing in the restaurant door, staring at him.

He waved at them, then with a laugh that didn't sound anywhere near as evil as he wanted it to, he walked off down the street, thinking about what had just happened and what it meant to his future.

Fortune Cookie Tyrant had taken his second step to world domination. He was coming to understand some of his powers and he knew he was going to enjoy using them. He just didn't know what exactly to do with them just yet.

FOUR

THE NEXT MORNING, Steven stared at the headlines in the morning paper as he sipped his morning coffee while sitting at the long counter in Larry's Diner and Deli.

Nude party breaks out in Chinese Restaurant.

The article said that no one really knew what happened, only that dancing nude in the street had sounded like fun and so they did it. Thirty-two people. Public indecency charges were pending.

Steven laughed and tossed the paper onto the counter. Being from a broken home and having been raised by his evil and uncaring aunt, Steven had very few morals. Normally, a nerd like Steven would have had few chances to push against what morals he did have. He had just assumed he would end up working some dead-end job, marry some woman who would go to fat after two kids, and die mostly broke with a bunch of grandkids arguing over his comic book collection.

But now it seemed he had a more promising future. He could run a big company, he could become a senator or even the president. Or he could just get very, very rich and live an easy life surrounded by beautiful women.

Or maybe he could do all those things.

"Why not?" Steven said out loud.

The guy two seats away down the counter said, "I agree. Why not?"

Steven glanced at him, then around at the diner. The cook, the waitress, and the five other customers were all staring at him, waiting for him to say something, like what he might say might be important.

Creepy. Having this kind of power over everyone around him might just get old. Then Steven laughed and said out loud, "That's not going to happen."

Everyone in the restaurant nodded. "You're right," the guy said beside him. "That's not going to happen."

He glanced at the waitress. "You sure you don't mind paying for my breakfast?"

She blinked, surprised, then smiled and said, "Not a problem."

"Thanks," he said, laughing and heading for the door.

This new power was going to be a lot of fun. But first, he had a lot of planning to do.

That afternoon, Steven went back to his apartment and started to do some research on the net. He needed to know how others had gained vast wealth and power if he was going to follow in their footsteps. He needed to know their

history, and the steps they took to keep the power.

And most of all, he needed to know what they did wrong. If he was going to get as much power as he was hoping to get, he needed to know how others lost theirs.

While running computer searches on different references to power, presidents, czars, dictators, and other tyrants through history, he came across a web site that was titled "The Top 100 Things I'd Do If I Ever Became an Evil Overlord."

The site was supposed to be a joke, aimed at all the bad clichés in Evil Overlords in fiction, but Steven knew better. The sight was a great reference guide to stop those who wouldn't follow him. Those two in that restaurant clearly haunted him, worried him more than he wanted to let on. And the top 100 things were rules all aimed at stopping those kinds of people.

Steven printed off the 100 rules and studied them carefully over the next few days. Most of the suggestions were things that would matter later in his climb to riches, power, and maybe even world control. He was starting to really think big.

But many of the suggestions in that list would help him on his rise to power. For example,

#4. "Shooting is not too good for my enemies."

Steven would always keep that firmly in mind, along with #24. "I will always maintain a realistic assessment of my strengths and weaknesses."

Then, after posting the list on the bulletin board in his kitchen, he took out the little slip of paper he had gotten from the fortune cookie and reread it one more time.

He needed to see if what he was thinking was right, that he had gotten his powers somehow from these fortune cookies. So he headed back to the Chinese restaurant he and Jane had eaten at the night before.

The employees were amazingly happy to see him as he came through the door, considering that most of them were facing charges for dancing nude and the restaurant was being investigated for spiking the food in some manner. Even with all that, there were still twenty people eating in the place and the moment he spoke to the man behind the front counter, they all stopped and turned to listen.

"I'd love to buy from you a large bag of your fortune cookies," Steven said.

"Here, take ours," one man at a table close by said, offering Steven their cookies. His wife was nodding, looking like a puppy trying to please a master.

"No, thanks," Steven said, waving the man off. "You two enjoy them."

Immediately the man and woman dug into the cookies, acting as if they were having small orgasms while crunching on the cookie, paper and all.

The man behind the counter grabbed a large bag that had to have three hundred fortune cookies in it. "This good?"

"That's perfect," Steven said. "And it's very kind of you to give them to me."

"The honor is ours," the man said.

Steven laughed as he left. It was getting easier and easier to just get everything for free. Whatever was happening with him, he sure loved it. He could get used to everyone waiting for him to talk. After all, that's what everyone did for those in power.

Back in his apartment, Steven opened the bag, got a glass of milk from the fridge, and cracked into the first cookie. It

was the same basic fortune that Jane had gotten the night before.

"You will come into a vast sum of money."

Steven laughed. "Yeah, that's going to happen."

A moment later, before he could even wash down the cookie with a sip of milk, the phone rang. He never did get back to the fortunes that day because his evil old aunt had had a stroke and was in the hospital. He didn't much like her, but he was the only thing she had. She died before he got there, which actually didn't upset him. Last thing he would have needed was the old bag hanging on and building up hospital bills.

He spent most of the night dealing with all the details of his aunt's death, then the rest of the night at Jane's, making her do things naked that no woman ever really thought of doing outside of porn films.

He sure loved his new power.

It was the next morning, after making funeral arrangements and talking to his aunt's attorney, that he came to understand what had happened. His aunt had left him everything, and the old broad had been rich. Millions rich, or so the attorney thought. It was still too early to tell just how much it might be.

Steven laughed all the way back to his apartment. Now he had his stake to get him started toward his plan of world domination. The cookie had been right again.

There was no telling what the next cookie would bring him. He could just keep opening cookies and gaining power.

Today, he would become a truly powerful being.

The bag of fortune cookies and the half-empty glass of old milk were right where he had left them. He dumped out the milk, got himself a fresh glass full, then took the first cookie off the top of the bag. He cracked it open, tossed half into his mouth, then read the fortune as he ate, as excited as a kid opening a present on Christmas morning.

But this fortune didn't seem right and he had to read it twice.

"All special powers that you have been given by fortune cookies will be forever lost."

Steven tossed the slip away like it was on fire, but it was too late. The feelings of being in control drained away from him like someone had pulled a plug in his shoe.

"No!" he screamed. "That's not a fortune!"

He slammed the rest of the uneaten cookie into the wall and grabbed another one from the bag, opening it and putting half in his mouth before reading the fortune.

It said the same thing.

And so did the next one and the next one.

He opened a hundred before giving up and sitting down on a stool in disgust.

Someone had planted the entire bag with the same fortune. But who? And why? And who would have known he was going to come back here and open all these?

A moment later the phone rang. It was his aunt's attorney again, talking some sort of gibberish about taxes and problems with the government and how there wasn't as much money as there had seemed to be earlier, maybe none at all after all the fees and hospital costs. Steven just listened in shock, said nothing, then hung up.

The money was gone as well, right along with his powers.

He stared at the kitchen counter covered in half-opened fortune cookies. He knew, without a doubt, he had lost everything, all his dreams of being in charge of everything.

But how? Why had someone done this to him, taken his specialness?

Then the faces of those two sitting in the Chinese restaurant came back clearly to mind. Not everyone would follow him. Someone had known what was happening, somehow, and had changed out his real cookies with these special ones.

He needed to find out who. And why.

He dumped the entire sack of cookies out on the counter. At the bottom was a note.

Dear Fortune Cookie Tyrant,

Steven stopped reading and sat down on the stool. That was a name he had only been thinking about using after he gained world domination. No one would know it now. Something wasn't right here.

Steven went back to reading the note.

You forgot rule #41. And sorry about the slow-acting and very painful poison in the cookies, but after what you did to the world over the last forty years, after all the people you killed and enslaved, we figured it was the least we could do.
Signed,
The Anti-Cookie Alliance.

Steven could feel the pain in his stomach starting to grow.

He swept all the cookies from the counter top, then doubled over in pain. He had been poisoned.

He got to the phone and dialed 911, begged for them to hurry, told the operator that the poison was in the cookies, then hung up as another wave of pain hit him.

As it eased, his mind went back to the note. Rule 41? What did the note mean by that?

And forty years? He was only twenty. He hadn't been alive yet for forty years.

In the distance, a siren was growling louder. Help was on the way.

Then he saw the list on his bulletin board, the list of 100 things he would do if he became an Evil Overlord. The list that he promised himself he would follow carefully.

With the pain in his gut causing him to stumble, he went to the board, pulled off the list, and slumped to the kitchen floor, his back against the wall. Outside his apartment, the sound of the siren stopped. He could see the flashing lights through the window.

Help would be here in a moment. He forced himself to take a deep breath to hold back the pain and flip the list to the right place.

Rule 41. Once my power is secure, I will destroy all those pesky time travel devices.

"No!" Steven shouted as the pain shot through his body. "I didn't get to become an evil overlord. I didn't get to be Fortune Cookie Tyrant."

There was a banging on the door and his name was called out.

He tried to get up, but instead went face forward onto the tile floor.

The last words the great Fortune Cookie Tyrant muttered was, "Not fair."

Now Available
from all your favorite booksellers
in trade paper and electronic editions.

USA TODAY BESTSELLING AUTHOR

DEAN WESLEY SMITH

WRITING INTO THE DARK

HOW TO WRITE A NOVEL WITHOUT AN OUTLINE

A WMG WRITER'S GUIDE

With more than a hundred published novels and more than seventeen million copies of his books in print, USA Today *bestselling author Dean Wesley Smith knows how to outline. And he knows how to write a novel without an outline.*

In this WMG Writer's Guide, Dean takes you step-by-step through the process of writing without an outline and explains why not having an outline boosts your creative voice and keeps you more interested in your writing.

Want to enjoy your writing more and entertain yourself? Then toss away your outline and Write into the Dark.

WRITING INTO THE DARK
A WMG Writer's Guide

Part 1 of 2

Introduction

In almost 150 novels now in both indie and traditional, I have written into the dark on some, done outlines on others, and even did a 135-page "fully realized" outline on one poor novel.

There are as many ways to outline a novel as there are writers. Plus, there are about a million books out there giving you the secret to outlining. In some of the online workshops I help with at WMG Publishing, I even taught a few ways to outline.

But there are very few articles and books on how to just type in the first word and head off into the dark writing a novel with no plan, no character sketch, nothing but pure exploration.

That's what writing into the dark is all about. Pure exploration of a story.

In this book, I hope to help you learn how to have the courage and the ability to just tell a story from your creative side.

SO WHAT EXACTLY IS WRITING INTO THE DARK?

Some call it "writing by the seat of your pants." There are other terms for it that are so stupid, I can't bring myself to even type the names of them.

Basically, writing into the dark means that you decide to write a story without an outline.

Now most short story writers do this automatically. But faced with a novel, the same writer who just had a blast going off into the dark on a short story will freeze down like a shallow lake in the Midwest in the dead of winter.

Critical voice takes over the writer's mind, and all the stuff the writer was taught by people who have never written a novel comes roaring in.

In fact, most of us in our early years of writing take all our information and learning from very, very unqualified people.

English teachers in high school may know how to put a sentence together in some grammatically correct fashion, but they have zero, or less than zero, idea how to create a story from nothing.

We are taught how to tear stories apart under the guise of learning, but that's like handing some kid a hammer and telling him to tear down a house. Then when the house is in rubble, you turn to the kid and say, "Now, build a wonderful new home with fine craftsmanship there."

The kid might have been fine at tearing a house apart, but tearing a house

down teaches little of the creative process, the building process.

So teachers tear apart a book, then make students outline the book. What that does is make the writer of the book look damn smart, actually. Students come away from the process thinking, "Wow, how did the writer know to put all that foreshadowing in chapter six for what's going to happen in chapter ten?"

So then, later, when the writer is facing a novel, the writer thinks all that idiocy taught in school is going to help the writer with the task of writing. Nope.

In fact, most of that learning from school will hurt the creative writer.

But off the writer goes, spending time and energy outlining and working on the outline and making sure the outline is perfect before ever writing word one. And all that is done from the critical voice, from the voice of a teacher who wouldn't have been able to write a novel on the threat of death.

Is it any wonder so many early outlined novels fail, and fail big time?

And actually, most outlined novels never get written. I'll talk about why later in the book.

CRITICAL VOICE VERSUS CREATIVE VOICE

A great deal has been said about critical voice versus creative voice in writing, or in any art, for that matter. Great art is rarely, if ever, created from a critical perspective. Art is never done purposely.

Great art comes from the creative side of our brains. I like to think of the creative part living in the back of our brains. The front part of our brains, the critical part, is what takes in all the information. The creative part has a large filter and only takes in the knowledge it wants and uses.

The creative side of our minds has been trained since we were born, and story has been trained into that creative side since we were first read to by our parents. The creative side loves story.

For most writers, the difficulty comes when trying to get past the critical side of our brains and write from the creative side only. Outlining comes from the critical side by the very nature of outlining.

So the critical side of our minds outlines a book, then we wonder why the creative side often doesn't want to follow the outline. The creative side knows story, knows what needs to be in a story.

So all the way through this book, I'm going to be talking about how to access the creative side, how to trust that part of your mind to create stories, and how to kill the fear that the critical voice will use to try to stop you.

Much, much more on this topic coming up.

WHY WRITE INTO THE DARK?

The first answer to that question is easy. Writing into the dark imitates the reading process for the writer.

All writers are readers. And as readers, we love it when a writer takes us along for the ride in a good novel.

So when writing into the dark, that same feeling of reading is in the writing process. Our conscious mind is just along for the ride. The creative side is making up a story and entertaining us as we type.

Later on in this book, I'll also talk about the many problems that stop outline writers. One major factor is boredom.

Imagine if every novel you picked up had a detailed outline of the entire plot, including the ending, right at the start. Would you read the novel after reading the outline?

Chances are, no. What would be the point? You already know the journey the writer is going to take you on.

So as a writer, why do an outline and then have to spend all that time creating a book you already know?

"Boring" doesn't begin to describe it.

And as I said, I wrote a lot of media tie-in books from outlines. My rule during those days was to write the outline, get it approved by Paramount or some other license holder, then never look at the outline and just write the book.

My memory is so bad that after seven to ten months from the time I wrote the outline to the time I got the contract and wrote the book, I had no memory of the book I had outlined at all. None.

And if the title hadn't been on the contract, I wouldn't have remembered that either.

So I never looked at the outline. Never. I just typed in the title and wrote off into the dark. That kept the book fresh and alive for me.

And no editor or license holder ever noticed the book was different from the outline they approved. Not once.

The key is to make a novel fresh to the reader. If the writer is bored or feeling like the book is "work" to write, you can bet that feeling is coming through the words to the reader.

Here is one more reason for writing into the dark: If you have no idea where the book is going, the reader sure won't either.

NO RIGHT WAY

Please remember, as I work through this book, that there is no right way of writing any particular book.

Or only one way for a writer to always work.

There are as many ways to write a book as there are writers.

Writing into the dark is just another option.

In the Thriller Online Workshop that I offer through WMG Publishing, numbers of writers mention to me each time that class is offered that they are surprised that I suggest character sketches and outlines.

And that I suggest taking another thriller writer's novel apart and outlining it to study.

There are some books, some projects, that would be better served with outlining.

No book is the same, no process is the same.

And I have to admit right here, in the introduction, that I outline in my own way, every book I write.

When I have a chapter finished, I jot down who the viewpoint characters are, what they are wearing, what happened in the chapter.

So as I go along, I outline each book as I write it.

I never outline ahead of the writing, but after the writing is done. That keeps the creative side of my brain in control of the writing.

And the real reason I do that is to keep track of what I have already done. And what a character is wearing. And so on.

It also helps my creative mind see the patterns in the book as I write.

So I write into the dark with most novels these days.

But I outline as I go, after I have written a chapter.

That's just my way. Use it if you want.

Now onward into how to get over the fear and critical voice problems that come with typing in a title and just writing a novel into the dark.

CHAPTER ONE
SOME BACKGROUND

THE REASON there are very few articles or books about writing into the dark is because the process gets such horrid bad press. Just the idea of writing without planning ahead on a project as long as a novel makes most English professors shudder and shake their head and turn away in disgust.

And beginning writers mostly just can't imagine doing that. It just seems impossible.

Yet, many long-term professional writers write this way. And many of the books those same English professors study were written completely into the dark.

So why do all of us, as we are growing up, buy into the idea that novels must be outlined to the last little detail to work?

First, the problem comes from the fact that we all started out as readers.

To readers, writers know it all. They know enough to make that plot twist work, that foreshadowing inserted at just the right place, the gun planted when it needs to be planted to be fired later, and so on.

To readers, writers are really smart to be able to do all that.

Then we get into school and all the English teachers build on that belief system by taking apart books and talking about the deep meaning and what the writer was doing. And that makes writers seem even smarter and the process of writing a novel even more daunting.

So the desire to outline is logical, totally logical, after all that.

In fact, it seems like outlining is the only way to do a complex novel.

But interestingly enough, that very process of outlining often kills the very complex structure the writer is hoping to achieve.

A HUMBLING EXPERIENCE

Two of the most humbling experiences in my life occurred the two times I went into a graduate-level English class at a university as a professional writer. (Do not do this if you can avoid it.)

The first time, the English professor, doing his job, had the students read and discuss two of my short stories BEFORE I GOT THERE.

So two of my stories were deconstructed by fifteen graduate English department students.

So I arrived, talked some about what it was like to be a freelance fiction writer, and then the professor turned the discussion to my two stories they had read. And I started to get questions about how did I know to put in the second hidden meaning of the story, or the foreshadowing of an upcoming event, or…or…or…

They all knew far, far more about those two stories than I did.

Honestly, I could barely remember the stories, and I had no idea I had even put in all that extra stuff they were all so impressed by.

And the reason I couldn't remember is that my subconscious, my creative brain, put all that in. My critical, conscious brain had nothing at all to do with it.

I had just let my creative brain tell a story.

Nothing more.

The problem was that for weeks after that first time into that class, I couldn't get all that crap back out of my head. I found myself wondering about second meanings, about subplots, about foreshadowing—all those other English-class terms. Froze me down completely until I got past it.

Let me be clear here. My critical brain is not smart enough to put all that stuff in. Luckily for me, my creative brain seems to be smart enough if I get my critical brain out of the way and let it.

But getting that stupid critical brain out of the way is the key problem.

BREAKING OUT OF THE TAUGHT PROBLEM

All of us go into writing novels with all that training of thinking we need to know all that stuff about subplots, foreshadowing, sub-meanings, and so on. Thinking about it, I find it amazing that with the training we get, any novel gets written at all.

Or that any writer even gets started writing.

And outlining seems to be the logical process when faced with all that. In fact, outlining would be the only way to let the critical brain even pretend to be smart.

When I started writing solidly, novels seemed flat impossible. I could manage a short story in an afternoon, but anything beyond that was a concrete wall of paralyzing fear.

So how did I break out of the problem of everything I had been taught?

I used to own a bookstore. One fine slow afternoon, I was sitting in the front room of my bookstore and I looked around at all the books in the room. And I had a realization that in hindsight sounds damn silly.

I realized that people, regular people, wrote all those books.

And what all those regular people did was just sit down and tell a story.

They were entertainers.

That simple.

It was no magic process that only really special English-department-anointed people could do. And if all those regular people with all those books covering the walls of my bookstore could do it, then I could do it as well.

So I looked at how I felt writing short stories.

At that point I just wrote a story and stopped when the story was over. Nothing more fancy. I figured I could do that with a novel as well.

So after that realization, over the next few years I started five or six novels and got stuck at the one-third point where I could no longer fight the critical voice into submission. I had no tools to fight the critical voice at that point in time, to be honest.

So two years after that realization, mad at myself for not finishing a novel and for making novels into something "important" instead of just fun, entertaining stories, I sat down at my trusty typewriter and thought only about writing ten pages a day.

I had no outline, nothing. My focus was on finishing ten pages.

Period.

Thirty days later I had finished an 80,000-word novel.

My first written novel.

The next day, I started into a second novel, doing ten pages a day again.

I powered my way through the need, the belief, the fear of doing a novel the way it "should" be done.

And never ever had that fear again. I had other fears, sure, but not that one.

Every long-term novel writer has some story of getting past the need for major outlines, for major planning. A lot of younger professionals are still banging out outlines and following them.

Again, no right way.

But eventually, if you are going to be around for a long time and writing, you need to feed the reader part of your brain and just write for fun.

Otherwise, knowing the ending of a novel, having it all figured out ahead of time, is just too dull and boring and way too much work.

CHAPTER TWO
THE CRITICAL VOICE PROBLEM

LET ME GIVE you a secret about writing.

Ready?

The only purpose of the critical voice in creative writing is to stop you.

That's the secret, and when you finally take that secret in, you will be on the way to really getting to your real writing ability.

Critical voice in humans is there to protect us.

In writing, it wants to stop you from making a fool of yourself, or from putting out a bad product. (Thus the intense desire to keep rewriting over and over.)

When your critical voice completely succeeds, you are no longer writing and sending out anything for others to read. After all, if someone else reads what you have written, it might be dangerous.

Made-up danger, of course, but to the writer letting the critical voice win, writing feels like very real danger.

In real life outside of writing, your critical voice is a protective mechanism.

In the late 1960s, I found myself standing on the top of a rock cliff near Sun Valley, Idaho, with two other skiers. We were looking at jumping off the cliff and there was a cameraman off to one side to take pictures.

My critical voice was screaming that we needed to check under the snow at the bottom for big rocks.

One of the other guys was suggesting the same thing.

Fear and critical voice had stopped us cold.

The third guy just shouted to the photographer to see if he was ready, then the guy backed up ten steps and skated at the cliff and went off into the air, ski tips down, arms spread, flying like a bird, laughing all the way.

The picture of him in the air off that cliff was in *Ski Magazine*. And he didn't hurt himself.

I skied around. So did the other guy.

The one guy in the picture went on to make a living in Hot Dogging, soon called Freestyle Skiing. He was fearless.

I let my critical voice combine with pure fear to stop me cold.

The best way many people see this concept clearly is in the bad horror movies when a woman in high heels goes into an old mansion where there is a killer. The woman in the high heels needs a better-developed critical voice.

No doubt about that.

(Or the writers need a new plot.)

But unlike going into an old mansion, or jumping off a cliff on skis, there is no danger in writing.

The fearless writers contain their critical voices and write what they love, what moves them.

As I said in the lecture on Writing into the Dark, my critical voice with writing is a tiny little thing whimpering off in a corner of my mind. When it tries to stand up, I throw bricks at it until it goes back to its corner and leaves me the hell alone.

WORK VERSUS PLAY

Writing from the critical voice is work. Plain and simple.

It's why so many beginning writers describe writing a book in metaphors that make them sound like they have just won a major world war all by themselves.

If I hadn't defeated my critical voice, I would have long ago moved on to doing something far more fun than writing from critical voice.

Writing without critical voice turned on, just writing to tell myself a story, is like reading. The process is wonderful and I enjoy the journey.

So what happens when a writer says out loud, "I'm going to write this next novel into the dark. No outline."

That is like giving your critical voice an energy drink or two. That critical voice will find a thousand ways to come at you.

I bet some of you while reading this have already had the critical voice yammering at you about how dangerous this would be.

Remember, the goal of the critical voice is to stop you.

Just remember my friend having his picture in *Ski Magazine* and me carefully and fearfully skiing around that cliff and you get the idea.

Throughout this book, I'm going to detail numbers of ways critical voice and fear will work to stop you, and how to get around them. But at this point I want to deal with one of the major ways that critical voice will come at you almost instantly when you even think of writing into the dark.

WASTED MY TIME

This is a huge killer, and I constantly hear this from new writers. Not only about writing into the dark, but about so many other aspects of writing.

Truth: When you are writing new words, you are never wasting your time.

Never.

Here comes a dirty word. Better cover your ears.

Practice.

There, I said it.

Imagine walking up to some poor kid who is practicing a musical instrument and telling that kid he is wasting his time by practicing. He needs to only play concerts or nothing at all.

Can't imagine that?

Yet when your critical voice tells you that you might be wasting your time, that's exactly what you are saying to yourself.

You are saying your writing must always be special, that it can't be done to practice.

Yeah, believing every word you write is always special will freeze you down into making writing work and then fairly quickly stop you completely.

And again, that's what the critical voice wants.

Critical voice does not want you writing or taking any chances. Period.

And writing into the dark? Wow, what a chance that would be. Far too much of a chance to take because your writing is "special." Your writing must always be perfect and maybe you had better add in just one more rewrite to be sure.

And maybe one more rewrite after that, because rewriting isn't wasting time.

That italics part, folks, was a sarcastic attempt to show you just how stupid those thoughts are. If you believe all of that was advice, you are beyond my help.

Truth: The biggest waste of time in writing is rewriting. Period.

But that's the topic of another book down the road.

Again, we're dealing with the sneaky critical voice always looking for ways to stop you. And rewriting is a great way.

AFRAID TO TRY

If you are afraid to try a new genre, afraid to try a new method of writing, afraid to try to get your work out to markets or show it to your friends, critical voice is in control and winning.

Period.

Heinlein's Business Rules from 1947 are really interesting when looked at from a defeating-critical-voice viewpoint.

Rule #1: You must write.

To do that, just that simple thing, you must overcome critical voice in many aspects.

Now Available
from all your favorite booksellers
in trade paper and electronic editions.

USA TODAY BESTSELLING AUTHOR

DEAN WESLEY SMITH

MORNING SONG

A SEEDERS UNIVERSE NOVEL

Rule #2: You must finish what you write.

Critical voice will keep you from finishing with a thousand tricks. If a story or novel isn't done, it can't be shown and thus can't cause you any (imaginary) harm.

Rule #3: You must refrain from rewriting unless to editorial demand.

Critical voice uses the myth of rewriting to make sure nothing will ever be "good enough" and ready to show anyone.

Rule #4: You must put your work on the market.

Critical voice can think of a thousand ways to make you afraid of the repercussions of mailing or indie publishing your work.

Rule #5: You must keep your work on the market until it sells.

Critical voice does wonders when you get rejections from an editor, and can stop you from putting the work back out. And if publishing indie, some imaginary expected sales figure not hit, or some bad review, will cause beginning writers to pull down work.

Heinlein's Rules of Business were to help writers get past critical voice. The rules really are that simple.

And because of critical voice, those five simple rules are almost impossible to follow.

Of course, your critical voice will instantly start coming up with ways how those rules don't apply to you.

Of course they don't.

Your critical voice knows best.

It knows how to stop you cold, keep you from writing.

That's its job, after all.

CHAPTER THREE
THE JOY OF UNCERTAINTY

I AM TRYING in these first few chapters to establish some basics that I hope will help you drive forward while writing into the dark.

The biggest factor once you get past the critical voice is uncertainty.

Uncertainty, when not controlled and used to push forward, causes problems.

Lots of problems.

When a writer lets uncertainty be a bad thing, it's like tossing open a window and inviting into your writing office all the fears and critical voice you can find. And once in, those fears and critical voice will slow you down and stop you.

Remember, that's their job.

Uncertainty, if looked at correctly and embraced, is a positive aspect of writing into the dark.

So let me battle in this chapter to help you keep that window closed to critical voice and fear. What I want to do is help you understand that uncertainty is a welcome feeling when writing into the dark.

THE BOREDOM FACTOR

From a reader's perspective, when I get to a spot in a book I know exactly how the book will end, I put the book down.

If Kris asks me what went wrong in the book, I say: "The book was on rails."

She'll nod because she understands.

The writer had placed the plot of the book firmly on a set of rails and the ending was as clear as knowing that the next stop on a train ride was the city ahead.

No uncertainty in the plot at all, and as a reader, I could see the ending of the book ahead.

So I got bored and put the book down.

Most readers are like me. Not all, but most.

When a reader realizes that they know how the book will end, they stop. It might not be a conscious thought. It might be just putting the book down to go get a cup of tea and never returning to the book.

The dreaded critique from a reader: "I knew what was going to happen."

How do you guarantee that statement will never, ever be made about one of your books?

Simple. Write into the dark.

Duh.

If you do not have one idea of where the book that you are writing is going, there is no chance in hell your reader will ever know.

Books on rails are books that were outlined. The writer knew exactly where the book was going, what the end was, so the writer's subconscious put in all the clues to tell the reader where the book was going, and everything in the book, every detail points to the ending like signs with arrows.

Books on rails are seldom original, either. Books outlined by the critical voice just can't be. The critical voice isn't your creative voice. Your critical voice can only dig up old ideas and old plots and parrot them back to readers already familiar with the plot.

So you are writing into the dark to stay original and you don't know where the plot is going.

How does that make you feel as a writer?

Uncertain, of course.

But if you want your book to be original and fresh and have no reader really know where it is going, you need to embrace that uncertainty feeling.

WHERE DO I GO NEXT?

I can hear the doubts, the questions.

If you don't know where the book is going, how do you know what to write next?

In the next numbers of chapters, that's going to be a major topic. I'm going to give you a bunch of ways of figuring that out.

But right here, early in the book, let me tell you the simple answer.

Write the next sentence.

And then write the next sentence.

I am not kidding.

It really is that simple.

What rule anywhere tells you that you need to know what is happening fifty pages away? No rule.

English teacher training or some such nonsense, more than likely.

Just write the next sentence that follows logically through the character from the previous sentence.

And repeat until you find the end of the story.

With every step of that path, with every sentence, uncertainty will be dogging you.

That's a good thing.

But at the same time, don't let the uncertainty be a fear-excuse to stop you writing.

Just write one more sentence. You can do it.

Then write one more sentence.

Repeat.

You know the drill.

It really does work.

UNCERTAINTY AS A SPORTING EVENT

For those of you who know me, know some of my past, you know I have been, and sometimes still am, an adrenaline junkie.

Professional hotdog skiing, professional golf, professional poker, jumping out of airplanes, rafting rivers, starting businesses, three wives, and so on and so on. Never a dull moment in my life, and I lived it that way purposely.

I sort of wonder at people with bucket lists. If there's been something I wanted to do, I just went and did it. I got nothing to put in some stupid bucket.

So here I sit getting adrenaline out of writing. I have fired into my own monthly magazine, I am building a new writing career at the age of sixty-four, and a new business as well.

So is it any wonder that the uncertainty of writing into the dark makes writing fun for me?

Adrenaline is everywhere, with everything I do, including all the learning I get from talking with writers on my blog.

I find the fear of not being able to come up with something to write great fun.

And you know, it's not often that sitting alone in a room and making stuff up can give you an adrenaline rush. (Queue all the porn jokes right here…)

I JUST DON'T KNOW WHAT IS NEXT

What happens when you can't even think of the next word to write, let alone the next sentence?

Your subconscious just won't let a word be written and you won't let your critical voice into the picture.

What do you do?

Again, in later chapters, I'm going to talk a lot more about all this sort of thing, how to get going again, and so on, but here, early in the book, I want to give you a basic writer trick you can use when that happens.

Sleep on it.

But before you call it a night, start off by taking a short break. Sometimes just five minutes will get you back to the next sentence.

And do not focus on how you need to end the chapter, or some plot thing. Just focus on trying to figure out what the character would do next.

What is the next sentence?

If you get back to the computer, do some methods I will outline later in the book, and the next sentence still doesn't come, then go take a nap.

Or go to bed.

The key to this is that as you stand up from the computer, tell yourself you'll have it figured out in the morning, or when you wake up.

Sometimes a five- or ten-minute nap will be enough for me to fire onward after being stuck.

However, the real problem with getting stuck like this is the uncertainty. Getting stuck, which will happen numbers of times in any novel or story, allows in all the doubts, the questioning of the very idea of writing into the dark.

It is getting stuck that causes so many writers to say, "I can't write into the dark. I always get stuck and then I have to outline."

Letting in your critical voice at that point is the worst thing a writer can do.

A writer must learn to trust the creative voice.

Sometimes that creative voice needs a little time, a short nap, a night's sleep, to get untangled, but it will get untangled if you keep the fear and critical voice away.

It is at that stuck point that you need to really embrace and enjoy the uncertainty.

Getting stuck is part of writing into the dark. It is part of the process, a natural part of the process of a creative voice building a story.

Embrace the uncertainty of being stuck, trust your creative voice, give it a few moments' rest, and then come back and write the next sentence.

What almost always happens for me after these rest points is that the book will power forward faster than I can type.

My creative voice has got it figured out and is off and running.

When a book does that, it's great fun.

Enjoy the adrenaline rush.

Remember that being stuck is normal.

And that this writing into the dark process is uncertain.

But one great side of writing into the dark: Your readers will never know the ending of one of your books.

CHAPTER FOUR
WHAT DO YOU NEED TO GET STARTED?

For this chapter, I'm going to go over a list of what you need to get started writing into the dark on a novel.

Some of these points are pretty basic, and some are more difficult.

But a simple list and explanation seemed to be the best way to get you at least mentally ready. All of these points will come up at different points throughout this book.

Be warned: Your critical voice will not like any of these. And if you find yourself disagreeing completely, you might not be ready yet to write off into the dark successfully.

You might be. But I wouldn't bet on it.

FIRST…YOU NEED A LOVE OF STORY

If you are still in that silly early stage of beginning writing where you think you need to read everything critically, you might not be ready yet to tackle a book into the dark.

By reading critically, you are feeding that critical voice with every sentence you read. And, of course, most stuff you read isn't good enough. That's the nature of the critical voice.

A writer like Cussler or Patterson or Nora Roberts or Grisham can entertain millions of readers with every book, and you and your overhyped critical voice will think they can't write at all. That's critical voice turned on far too high and your ego far, far out of control.

You must get back to reading for enjoyment, for the sheer love of a good story told well.

You won't like all books, but your dislike will be for taste, not critical voice. And that's fine.

So if you haven't read a book lately and gotten so lost in the story that you haven't seen a word of the book, then writing into the dark might not be such a good idea until you can get back to really loving to read for the sheer pleasure.

When you can read a book and not see a word of type, then you are ready.

And if you automatically copyed-it everything you read, go get help. And I mean real help, professional help, because you have lost all ability to see a story and are trapped by the little black marks on the paper. You can't even begin to be a writer from that mindset, let alone a creative writer, let alone write into the dark.

But if you enjoy story, love to read, and can't see the words when reading because you are lost in the story the writer is telling, you will be fine moving forward and into the dark with your writing.

SECOND...EARLY PRECONCEPTIONS CLEARED

All those preconceptions of the need to consciously put in foreshadowing or plot arcs or character threads or rising and falling tension. You know, all that English class crap you were taught by people good at deconstruction but shitty at creative work.

You must have most of that cleared out, or at least under control in your mind. It is why I talked about it early on in this book.

Studying books, studying plot threads, studying rising and falling tension is one thing for writers to do *after* they read a book and like it.

But you can't come at a book, ready to write a book, with the idea you are going to put that all in.

You have to know that the desire to consciously put in all the literary crap is your critical voice, the thing that is out to stop you cold.

For writing into the dark, the critical voice needs to be ushered into a closet and the door slammed until the book is done.

Your creative voice will put all the stuff that needs to be there in the book, and make you look really, really smart to English classes later. And as I discovered, you won't even know you put that stuff in there for those deconstructionists to find.

But to actually give your creative voice permission to put that all in, you need to take all that sort of stuff out of your critical mind. Focus on only having fun telling a story.

Be prepared to just let the creative voice have its day.

Really hard to do.

Impossible to do if you are reading critically.

THIRD...YOU NEED TO UNDERSTAND YOU WILL WRITE EXTRA

When writing into the dark, the story will often come in parts, and sometimes the parts aren't in a real order. That's part of the fun. And later on in this book I'll explain how to deal with all that.

Sometimes, like a reader, you experience the writing process from word one to the last word. But sometimes, like a cave explorer, you have to see what is up a certain cave until it dead-ends into a rock wall. Since you are walking into the dark, a dim flashlight your best guide to see the step ahead, you won't know until you find the dead-end that you were on the wrong track.

That's normal.

And sometimes what you find on that little side trip is valuable to the story and your subconscious took you up that path for a reason. Again, never let the critical voice in to second-guess the subconscious. Just be prepared to accept writing some extra.

For me, in many books, I write very little extra. But for some reason, in my Thunder Mountain series, I tend to write a lot extra.

I have two reasons for that. One is that I am used to writing those bloated, longer books under contract that New York wanted me to write. And to get a story up to length, I would often have to just add in plot sidetracks.

I hated that, and with my own books, I won't do that. A story is as long as a story needs to be.

Period.

But with Thunder Mountain, complex time travel Westerns, I love the setting and the time period, so I have often put my characters on their horses and thought "Wow, wouldn't it be fun to go off the trail and see what's over there?"

(I like doing that in real life as well, but since I have stuck Kris in wilderness areas one too many times, I can now only do that when I am alone in the car.)

What happens in my novels then is that when I am done, my sidetracks are just things I put in for myself. No plot reason, and my subconscious says, "You had your fun, get that out of my story now."

So in that series, I often write a bunch of side roads just for myself.

And I accept that and enjoy it.

Expect to write extra, for whatever reason, when writing into the dark.

FOURTH...YOU ARE NOT GOING TO REWRITE THE BOOK

That's right.

Do not give yourself permission to fix anything later.

Do not give yourself permission to write sloppy.

The First Two Cold Poker Gang Novels
Available at your favorite booksellers.

You are writing a book. Period. When you are done writing, you release the manuscript to your first reader and proofreader and move on to the next story you want to tell.

I will explain later in this book some ways to help you produce clean copy as you go along. But you cannot allow your critical voice in any fashion to get anywhere near the book you are writing into the dark.

You can't allow that critical voice to glare in the window, saliva dripping from the teeth, just waiting to get hold of the poor manuscript. That's a quick way to make writing into the dark worthless.

And that includes permission from the critical voice to write sloppy or a second draft.

Otherwise there is no reason to write into the dark. You just might as well outline the poor, sad book and let the critical voice kill it that way.

Yeah, I know, I can hear the screaming now.

And why are you screaming???

Really ask yourself that question. Why are you objecting?

Critical voice, right?

All those English teachers taught you that rewriting is the only way to create real art. Those teachers who couldn't write a creative sentence if forced at gunpoint. Those same ones.

And you bought into that myth.

So answer one simple question: Why you do not believe that you, the creative writer, can write a book from the creative side of your brain without that critical voice pissing all over it?

As I said a moment ago, later in this book I will show you some methods on how to produce clean copy as you go so that when you get to the end, you re-

lease and start thinking about the next story.

But for most, this will be the hardest part of writing into the dark.

There is no point at all of writing into the dark if you are going to give your critical voice permission to ruin what you did.

And that permission will kill all the enthusiasm of the creative side as well.

And the entire process will fail.

All because you bought into a myth and believe your creative brain just isn't good enough.

Sad, really sad.

CHAPTER FIVE
HOW TO GET STARTED

One of the established facts of novel writing is that almost no writer can hold the plot of an entire novel in their mind. We just can't.

So even if you are outlining ahead, you are spending most of your time just focusing in on one area of the book, one scene, one chapter.

I have a reminder on my wall above my computer:

Write Scenes

That sign was meant to keep me from trying to think about an entire book, or too far ahead in a book.

The sign under the first sign is:

Trust The Process

Can't believe how many times I repeat that to myself when feeling uncertain.

Trust the process. Just trust the damn process.

It's like a signal to my subconscious to come out and play.

That's all fine and good, but how to get started with the actual writing? That seems to be the scary question we all face with every book or story.

SOME ACCEPTED WAYS

In writing book after writing book on this topic, the same basic answers come up about getting started.

They all say that you need one or more of the following:

—An idea

—A cool setting

—Cool character

—Great first line

Okay, those sometimes help. For me, a cool title helps as well.

But if I had to wait around for a cool idea or a cool first line like Billy Crystal in that movie *Throw Momma From the Train*, I would be dead.

So sure, all those things help. But then what?

How do you really get started?

For the answer to that, let me back up to the basics of every opening in any story or chapter.

You must have a character in a setting.

Readers read for characters and all characters must be in something besides a white room.

So to get started, stick a character in a setting. Cool character or not. Cool setting or not.

Just a character in a setting.

Period.

Sounds simple, doesn't it?

Nope. Far, far from it.

THE DEPTH WORKSHOP

The most important and successful workshop I do through WMG Publishing Online Workshops is the Depth Online Workshop.

Here is how to think of depth when writing openings.

Imagine a lake. All beginning writers just try to get their readers to go out across the top of the lake. But the surface of that lake is the line that allows a reader to leave your story. If the reader gets above that surface line, they put the book down.

A simple image.

A story with depth is one that the writer takes the reader and drags the reader under the surface and down the steep slope to the bottom of the lake. And then the writer has the reader follow the story along the bottom of the lake.

From the bottom of that lake, it is a long way to the surface and the writer can do all sorts of things without fear the reader will surface and leave the story.

So the worst thing you can do it just let your readers waterski across the top of the water. You want your readers deep in your story, with no chance they will leave.

That is called depth.

And it takes me six weeks and five assignments and a ton of examples to show writers how to do that in that Depth Online Workshop.

So back to the question on how to start a story.

Take a reader quickly down into depth.

Those who have taken the online workshop know how that's done.

For everyone else, let me just say this:

Depth is caused by having a character be firmly in a setting with opinions and all five senses and emotions about the setting.

None of this can be from a writer's perspective.

It all must be inside a character's head.

AN EXAMPLE

A few months back I wanted to write another Thunder Mountain series time travel novel. I always start those novels with new characters, but I had no character, no idea of a character, nothing. I just had a title: *Lake Roosevelt.*

Roosevelt Lake is a lake in the center of Idaho with a town under it. All the Thunder Mountain books had been around that lake in one form or another, so I figured it was time to call one of the books by the lake name. Thus the title.

So I sat down, typed in the title, and grabbed a character name out of a phone book from some faraway city and typed in that as the first two words of the story.

And since I live on the Oregon Coast I figured why not just set the opening here? That thought flashed across my mind from somewhere unknown.

So I started typing. I had the character enjoying the fantastic beauty of the Oregon Coast and going into a small café in a small Oregon Coast town.

Café had great smells, of course. Great tastes, the ocean air, the sounds of the waves, and the warmth of the late summer day. I had all five senses and I layered them in really thick, giving my character's opinions of the setting with hints of what she was doing there.

Character.

Setting.

Then I ended the chapter and did the same thing with a male character in chapter two who was following the first character.

Character.

Setting.

And it went from there.

I stuck two characters in two chapters in rich, thick settings that they had opinions about.

Did I know where the book was heading? Nope, other than I figured at some point they would make it back to Idaho.

Did I know the characters? Nope, just learning about them as I typed.

Just as a reader would learn about them as the reader reads the book.

HOW TO GET STARTED WRITING INTO THE DARK

Take any character and put the character in a setting.

Any character.

Any setting.

Then climb into the character's head and park your butt there and don't allow yourself to type one word that doesn't come from the character's opinion or sensory feelings or emotions.

Stay parked inside that character's head.

And let the character (and the reader) experience the story.

To be continued...

Now Available

from all your favorite booksellers
in trade paper and electronic editions.

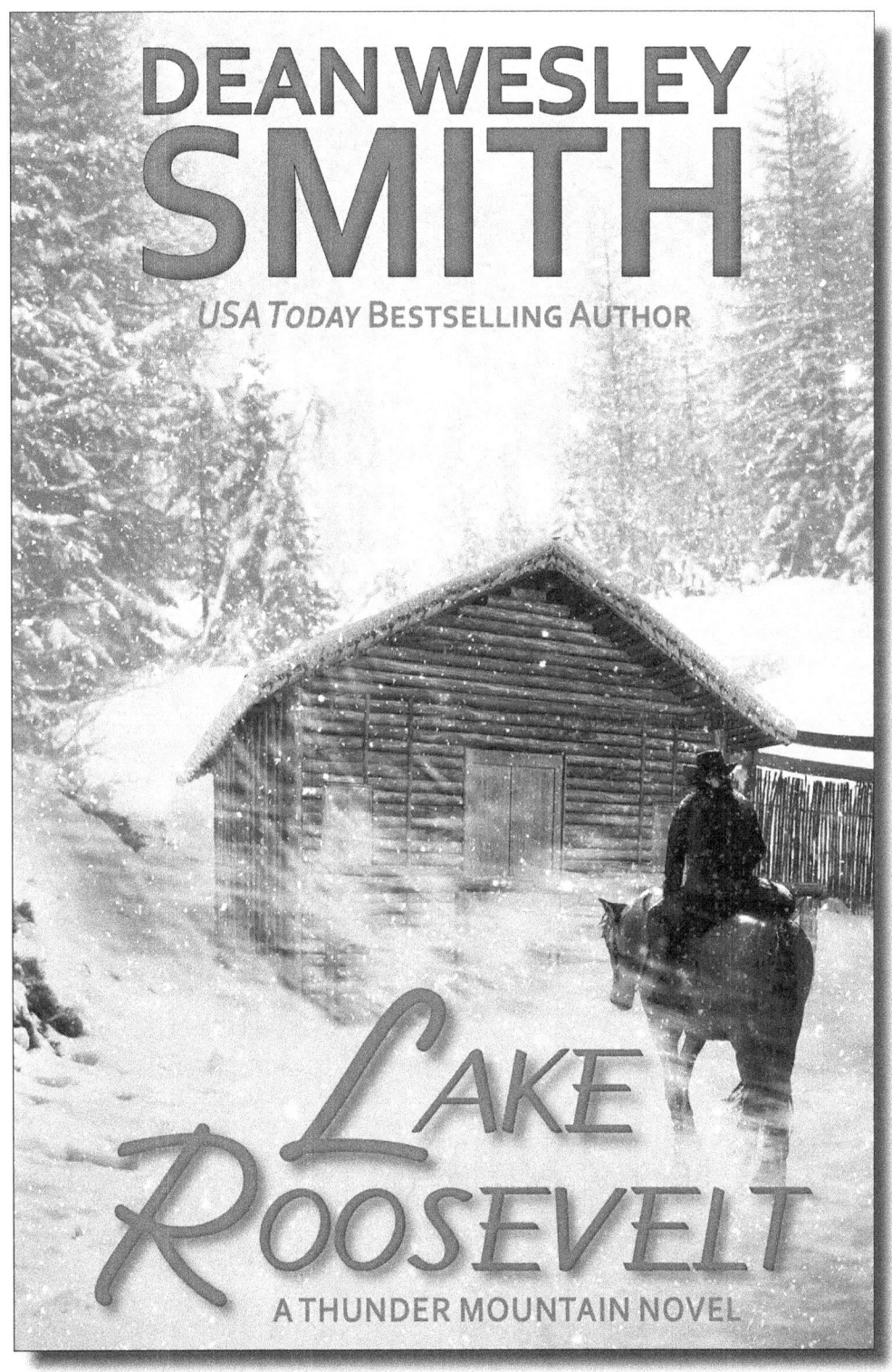

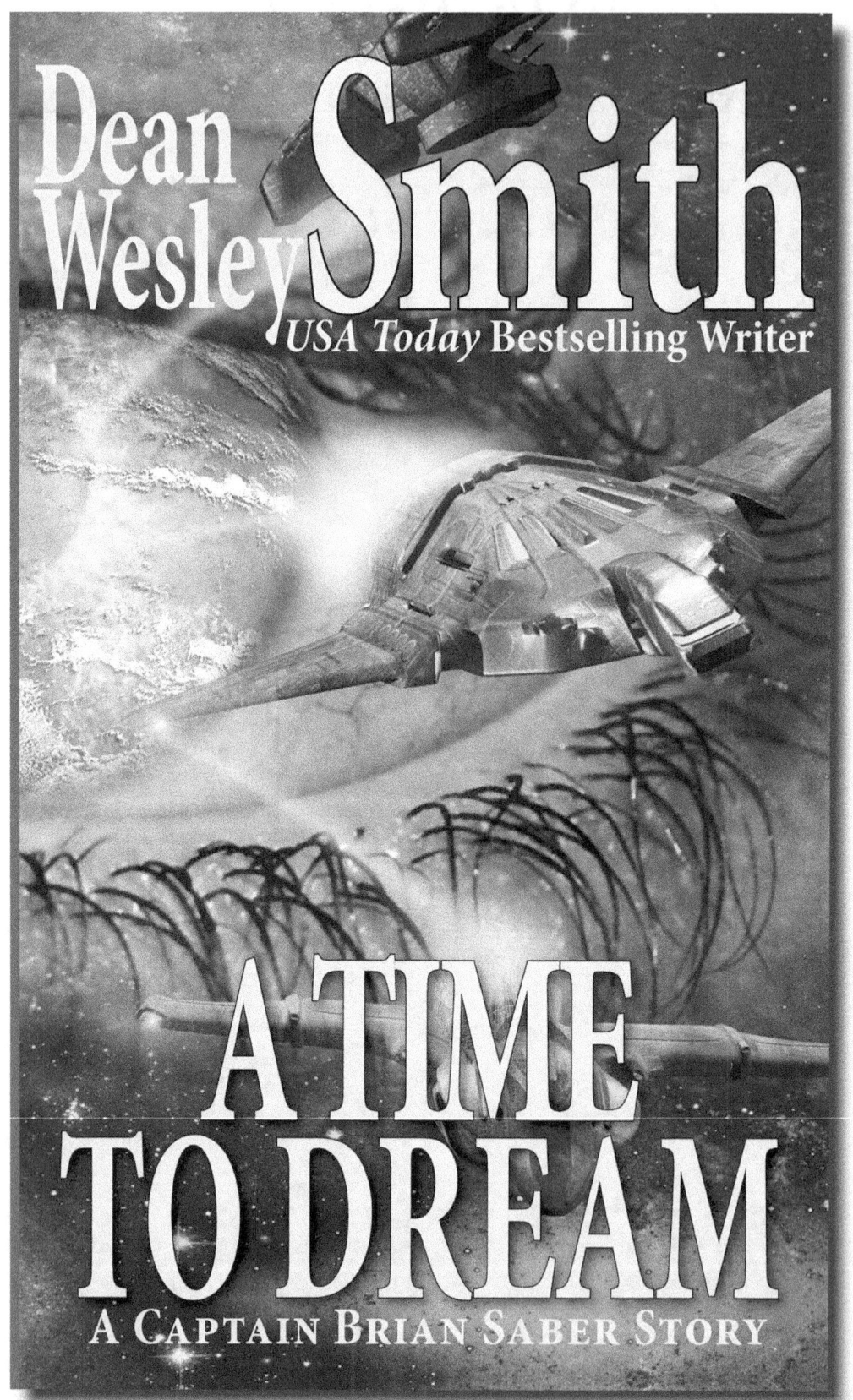

Dean
Wesley Smith

USA Today Bestselling Writer

A TIME
TO DREAM

A CAPTAIN BRIAN SABER STORY

Captain Brian Saber, his ship and other Earth Protection League ships face a suicide mission to save Earth.

Can he succeed, even though seemingly moments before he lay slowly dying of old age in a nursing home on Earth?

The first Captain Brian Saber story.

A TIME TO DREAM
A Captain Brian Saber Story

ONE

CAPTAIN BRIAN SABER of the Earth Protection League could tell there would be a mission. Tonight was the night. The first mission in over a week. The border skirmish on the third moon of the Garland Star Cluster must have flared up again. Or something else threatened the security of Earth. The League was needed to stop the threat. He was needed, and he was ready.

Across the small nursing home room the old clock on the wooden dresser ticked, echoing in the small space and dim light, demanding his attention just as it did every night as he lay in his bed, awake, waiting. When he'd first arrived at the Shady Valley Nursing Home outside of Chicago six years earlier after his second stroke, that old clock had let him count down the seconds until he died. Long seconds, never-ending seconds that he had wished would go by faster.

Now the loud ticking in the night of that old clock counted the minutes until the next mission, until the time he could become young again. And the time waiting, getting older and closer to death went by too fast now.

Far too fast.

Now he wanted to stay alive, to stay with the missions and the Earth Protection League, to get the chance to be young enough to wear his Proton Stunners and fight the good fight against the enemies of Earth.

The clock ticked.

Time went by.

Down the dimly lit hall outside his room's door a nurse laughed at an unheard joke. Captain Brian Saber coughed, the sound weak and pitiful in the silence of the nursing home.

He glanced at the clock. He could barely see the hands in the light from the hall, but he could tell it was only a little after ten in the evening. It was still far too early for them to come for him.

He tried to roll his eighty-three-year-old body over on its side, but only succeeded in shifting the sheet slightly under him. He hadn't had the strength to pull himself out of bed for over two years, let alone roll over. And he couldn't remember the last time he'd walked across this small room on his own to the bathroom. A nurse's aide always had to carry him and plop him on the cold toilet, then carry him back to his bed or wheelchair.

The small strokes had just kept eating at him, taking parts of him bit-by-bit. The doctors said they had them under control now, at least.

He laughed, and the laugh again turned into a rough cough that sent his old heart pounding. He forced himself to calm down and to not think about how he was at the moment. He hated thinking about how old he was, how frail his body had become, how dependent on others he now was. He reminded himself that none of that mattered like it used to.

Now he had the missions for the Earth Protection League. The missions gave his old life purpose, his continued living in this way station of the dying a valid reason. And even though there hadn't been a mission for almost a week, he knew tonight was the night.

He could tell.

It was all in the details. For example, the night nurse had left the rail on his bed down. The nurse never did that, except on mission nights.

They had also cleaned him up early and put him to bed. They never did that either unless there was a mission to run.

Of course, when he had first talked to them about the missions after his first one, they had all laughed at him. They had said there was no such thing as the Earth Protection League. They claimed that he had just had a strange dream.

But he knew better.

He'd gone on a mission, gotten young again. He had helped Earth defend itself against the evil scum of the galaxy. And since that night he'd gone on many, many more missions.

Tonight he was ready again.

Hell, he was always ready. There was nothing else for him to do.

The clock ticked the night away minute by minute, second by second. On the night of a mission, waiting was the hardest. Sometimes he wished he couldn't tell when a mission was. It would make sleep easier.

So he forced himself to think about other things. First he thought about his long-dead wife, Margaret. She would have laughed at him if she knew what he was doing. But she wouldn't have minded. She had always supported him in everything he did, one of the many things he had loved about her.

Their children, Strom and Claire didn't have time for him much anymore. They didn't even live close and had their own lives, their own jobs, their own kids to raise. He hadn't bothered to even hint to them about the missions. There would have been no point. They were part of his past. None of that compared with his life now as a Captain in the Earth Protection League.

He watched the clock as it ticked away the time.

At some point along the way, at least an hour after midnight, he dozed off.

TWO

"CAPTAIN SABER?" the young, male voice said.

Strong arms picked him up from the bed and moved quickly toward the sliding glass door that led into the center court of the nursing home. "We need your help again, Sir."

"Always ready to help," Saber said. His old vocal cords managed to barely choke out the words. Those were the same words he always said at the start of every mission.

He glanced at the old clock on the way out. Three-sixteen in the morning. He would be back shortly.

If he lived.

The sliding door to the outside was open and the Chicago night air was cold against his old skin. But the young soldier who carried him didn't even pause. He strode across to the center of the court and then tapped a badge on his wrist. A white beam of light from above lifted them quickly into the transport ship.

Saber knew that around the country the same thing had happened, or was happening, at least forty-one other times as his crew was gathered from their respective nursing homes and retirement apartments.

The young man with the strong arms quickly moved to a silver, coffin-shaped

sleep chamber and laid Saber down slowly on the soft cushions.

"Any hints as to the fight?" Saber asked. "The nature of the mission?"

The young soldier smiled. "Couldn't tell you if I knew, sir," he said. "But they never tell us grunts what's happening on this end. I just wish I could be there with you."

Saber laughed. "I wish you could, too, son."

But both of them knew that wasn't possible. The reason the eighty-three-year-old Saber was going instead of the young soldier was because of the problems with Trans-Galactic flight. Simply put, it regressed a human body. If that kid had come along, he'd be nothing more than a baby, if that, when they dropped out of Trans-Galactic flight.

And so far no one could figure out why it did that, or so he was told. He had heard all the explanations of relativity, the curved nature of space, and the different fixed states of matter, but it still had made no sense to him.

All he knew was that he was old when the flight started and young again when it ended. The farther and faster the ship flew, the greater the distance from Earth, the younger he got. Then, when he came back to Earth, due to the fixed nature of matter in relationship to space and time, his body got older again.

Or at least, that was what he understood happened when they tired to explain it to him. It must have been very strange for whoever invented Trans-Galactic flight that first time, discovering that a person's age totally depended on their location in space and time.

He often wondered if the Earth Protection League had a group of middle-aged soldiers for shorter-range work, but he had never been in a position to ask anyone.

He was just glad space flight worked this way.

The young soldier patted his shoulder. "Have a good trip, sir." Then he closed the lid on the coffin and tapped it twice as a signal to Saber that it was secure. In this old body, it didn't matter. He wouldn't have been able to even push the lid open if he tried.

A moment later the rose-smelling gas filled the chamber and he drifted off into the sleep of the dead as the Trans-Galactic ship jumped out of Earth orbit and headed toward the center of the Galaxy.

THREE

THE TOP OF the coffin snapped open with a hiss and cool oxygen bathed over his face. Captain Brian Saber snapped his eyes open, then held his arms up to look at them. What he saw was the young skin and shapes of youth. He flexed his fingers and the muscles under the skin rippled.

It felt wonderful!

No pain, no aches. Just the sense of health and youth.

Yes! He had made it again.

With both hands he grabbed the sides of the sleep module and lifted himself out, kicking over the side without so much as a caught heel. The feeling of youth was simply wonderful.

He still wore his old man's night-gown, but he quickly pulled that off and tossed it back in the coffin. He'd need it for the return trip, if he lived through this coming fight. If not, they'd need it for his body. And tomorrow morning his kids

would get a call that he had died peacefully in his sleep.

He flexed the muscles in his shoulders and neck. His body was one he barely remembered from his youth. Yet each time he went on a mission, this body returned, good as ever. Whatever the strange relative-matter-physics involved in Trans-Galactic travel, he loved this body.

Quickly he dressed in his uniform of the Earth Protection League. First the leather pants and high boots, then a silk blouse that flared under his arms and fit tight over his shoulders. Next he put on a leather vest over the blouse that had the EPL triangle symbol on the chest. Then he strapped on his twin Photon Stunners, one on each hip.

Brushing a hand through his full head of dark hair, he turned and glanced at the only mirror in the small room. The reflection that greeted him was one of his youth, control, and power. He couldn't be more than twenty-one or twenty-two. Only the knowledge and memories inside the young body were of the old man who had, seemingly moments before, been asleep in a nursing home room just outside of Chicago.

He patted the Stunners on his hips, then with one more quick look in the mirror, he turned and strode out of the room, turning right toward the Command Center of the Galactic-Transport ship. He knew this ship like the back of his young hand. He'd been on board it for dozens of missions now, had flown it through some of their toughest space in this sector of the Galaxy. It felt like home, far more than his home back in Chicago had ever done.

Throughout the ship his men would be awaking, dressing, getting ready for whatever faced them tonight. He didn't wait for them, but instead strode directly to the empty Command Center and dropped into the Captain's chair.

His chair.

Around him there was only one other station on his left, with a high-backed chair like his and view screens above it showing the blackness of space.

In front of him a small screen on the panel flared to light and the smiling face of General Datson Meyers filled it. He had deep blue eyes, white hair, and more wrinkles than almost any human Saber had ever seen. Yet the face was one that seemed comfortable with command. "Glad you made it, Captain Saber."

"Glad to be here, sir," Saber said. "What's happening?"

The smile cleared from the face of the General, making some of the wrinkles vanish instantly. "The Dogs have broken through."

"What?" Saber said, stunned. The Dogs, as everyone in EPL called them, were a race of ugly aliens that occupied the territory along one of the EPL's borders. They looked like a bad cross between a huge slug and a ten-legged poodle. They were the meanest damn things Saber had ever fought, and he had fought them often along that border.

Unlike the dogs on earth, humans and alien Dogs hated each other with a passion that didn't allow any type of agreement beyond fighting.

The general went on. "They broke through our outer defenses yesterday. Our allies in the League and border patrols couldn't stop them."

"That bad, huh?" Saber asked. A feeling of dread was quickly replacing the wonderful feel of being young again.

The general nodded. "This morning we got data that leads us to believe that they are headed to Earth to destroy the center of the League once and for all."

Saber looked intently at the general, not letting the worry filling his chest show. "How many ships did they send?"

"Over five hundred got through the border and are headed for your position at a slow Trans-Galactic speed," the general said. "Your job is to try to slow them down even more, give us time behind you to form a second and third line of defense."

"Understood," Saber said. "We'll slow them down. Maybe knock their numbers down a few. You can count on that."

The general nodded. "I knew I could depend on you, Captain."

The screen went blank.

Saber sat there in the command chair, stunned. This would be the last mission. He would die young and in deep space, just as he had always hoped he would. Better than in his sleep in the nursing home back on Earth. He just hadn't expected this last mission to be so soon.

But Earth and the League needed him. He would not let them down!

He took a deep breath, shoved the fear aside, and got to work.

Quickly he ran his fingers over the controls in front of him. It showed that there were eleven other League ships in formation beside his. And each ship was manned with forty-two people like him and carried forty single-man fighters. One of the big transport ships might be a match for a single Dog Warcraft, but a single-man fighter wasn't. It would be like sending a mosquito after a real dog back on Earth.

"What are we up against this time, Captain?" a cheery voice asked behind him.

He glanced over his shoulder at his second in command, Carl Turner. Carl lived in a nursing home in northern California and was gaining on one hundred years of age. At the moment he was a brown-haired man who looked like he was in his middle twenties. He had a spring in his step and a smile that could light up a room, and often did. They had worked dozens of missions together before and had become best friends.

"The Dogs broke out of their fence," Saber said. "We're supposed to try to slow them down until the League can mount a decent defense behind us."

"Shit," Carl said as he dropped into the chair beside Saber and stared at the screen. "How many?"

"Five hundred of their warships. Twelve of us."

"The League have any idea how we're supposed to do this?" Carl asked.

"Nope," Saber said, smiling at his friend. "They left it up to our ancient wisdom to come up with something."

"I hate it when they do that," Carl said.

"Yeah, me too," Saber said, laughing. "You work on finding out how much time we have until they get here, what speed they're moving, so on, and I'll brief the rest of the crew."

He pushed himself easily to his feet and strode across the command center toward the crew area. He could have done this task from his command chair, but he wanted to feel young again, walk quickly again, just one more time.

FOUR

IT WAS HALFWAY through the briefing with the forty members of his gathered crew that Captain Brian Saber came up with the plan that just might save them. And Earth.

He sprinted back to the Command Center of the ship and dropped back into his chair. "How long?"

"Five hundred Dog Warships will be on our front steps in exactly thirty-five minutes."

"Perfect," Saver said. "Have our ships get ready to match their Trans-Galactic speed."

Carl glanced over at him. "Perfect if you like getting your butt kicked by slug-looking poodles."

"How old are you, Carl?" Saber asked, his fingers working on the board as he talked.

"Six months short of the big one hundred," Carl said.

"And how long did it take us to get from Earth to this position?"

"From what measuring point?" Carl asked.

"Earth time?"

"Forty or so years," Carl said.

"Shipboard time?"

"Six days, ten hours, and a few odd minutes."

"And it will take us that long to get back?" Saber asked, "Right?" He finished the work on the command board and turned to Carl.

"Shipboard time," Carl said. "They'll speed up the ship slightly on the return voyage and we'll end up back in our beds less than thirty minutes after we left, Earth time that is. You know that."

"So how are the Dogs handling the same matter/relativity problem on their flight toward Earth?"

"How the hell would I—"

Suddenly Carl stopped and smiled at Saber. "I see where you're headed

Captain. Their life spans are shorter than ours, right?"

"Exactly," Saber said. "Which is why they are moving at a slow Trans-Galactic speed, because they don't dare go any faster or they would end up Dog-pups when they reached Earth."

"Which means they have to be damn old Dogs right now," Carl said, "at the beginning of their flight."

"Exactly," Saber said. "And you and I both know how well old dogs like us move."

Carl laughed. "We're young, they're old. You're right! Perfect!"

"I'd say it's time to kick some wrinkled butt, don't you?" Saber asked. He punched the communications link to all his men and the other ships. Quickly he explained what he had figured out and how they were going to fight the Dogs.

"Keep the single-man fighters on full thrust and constantly turning, diving, retreating. We'll break into units of twenty fighters with each twenty-ship unit attacking one Dog ship, then moving on. Keep moving as fast as you can, all the time. They're slow and old, just as we all were a few short hours ago. Remember that and they won't stand a chance."

Twenty minutes later they launched the single-man fighters. Only Carl and Saber remained in the Command Ship, since it only took the two of them to run the ship. Everyone else was needed in the fighters.

A few minutes later the Dog Warships appeared on the view screens. They were ugly, sausage-looking ships, with slick-looking hulls and protruding weapons systems and thrusters. The fighters had been ordered to stay away from in front of the weapons and target the thrusters. Their mission was to slow them down

and, as Carl said, there was no better way to do that than shoot a Dog Warship in the ass.

"You know how to override the auto-pilot on this ship?" Saber asked, turning to Carl as the fighters broke into groups and swarmed toward the oncoming Dog Warships.

"I think I could do it?" Carl asked. "Why?"

"I'm just wondering," Saber said, "what would happen if we plowed right through the middle of that fleet at full Trans-Galactic speed?"

"Besides destroy us?"

"Won't hurt us," Saber said. "At full Trans-Galactic speed we're on complete screens, big enough to knock just about anything out of the way. Remember?"

Carl stared at Saber for a moment, then laughed. "Bowling for Dogs. I love it!"

Carl set to work on taking the auto-pilot off the Trans-Galactic controls.

On the screen the fighters were having some luck. The Dog Warships were firing, but not really hitting anything. The fighters were picking at the thrusters of the ships like a kid picked at a scab. Two Dog ships were already dead in space, left behind by the fleet. But there were already four single-man fighters destroyed. Four men who wouldn't be returning alive to their nursing home rooms tonight on Earth.

Saber wondered if any of them would be at this point.

"Got it! Carl said.

Saber carefully set the Trans-Galactic drive for only a sixteen second burst. That would take them through the Dog Warship fleet and some distance beyond, but not too far. Too far and they'd be too young to pilot the ship back into position.

Quickly he informed the other transport Captains of what he was going to try to do, then turned to Carl. "Ready to lose a little time?"

"And with luck, a few Dog Warships in the process," Carl said.

Saber eased the transport directly at a mass of the Dog Warships, then said, "Do it!"

Carl flicked the switch and for the first time in all the missions, Saber saw what space looked like at full Trans-Galactic speed.

It was a blur of black and white streaks.

Nothing more. Not even pretty.

Then as quickly as it started, it ended and the stars were back, solid in space. There was no sign of the Dog Warships, or the rest of the League transport fleet.

"We've gone almost to the Dog Border and we're four weeks younger than a few seconds ago," Carl said.

"I knew I felt better," Saber said. "Don't you just love how this relativity and mass and matter stuff works?"

"Yeah," Carl said. "Just wish I understood it."

"I hear you there," Saber said.

Saber flipped the ship over and with a quick run of his fingers over the board reset the controls to return them to just a few seconds after they had left.

"Do it," he said.

"Firing for the return!" Carl said.

Again the view screens showed black and white streaks for a long six seconds, then normal space returned.

"Holy cow!" Carl said. "I think we got a strike."

"Maybe two," Saber said, staring at the damage they had done. They had punched not just one, but two holes in the fleet of Dog Warships, damaging and destroying at least thirty of them.

And the single-man fighters were taking advantage of the confusion to cause even more damage.

"Tell the other transport Captains exactly what we did and then let's go again," Saber said.

"They're going to come up with a terrible name for this, you know," Carl said.

Saber had already reset the Trans-Galactic drive for another six-second burst and aimed the nose of the ship at a mass of the Dog Warships. "And what would that be?"

"The Saber Yo-Yo Maneuver," Carl said.

"Sounds good to me," Saber said, laughing as he punched them back into full Trans-Galactic speed once again. And for a few seconds, he got even younger again.

FIVE

THE FRESH-FACED SOLDIER carried the frail frame of Captain Brian Saber out of the cold of the Chicago night air and into the warmth of the small nursing home room, then laid him carefully on the bed.

Saber glanced at the clock. Three thirty-seven in the morning. He'd only been gone just a little over twenty minutes Earth time, yet for his memory it had been much, much longer.

It had taken him and the other eleven transport ships six more punches through the Dog Warship fleet before the Dogs finally gave up and turned back.

They had chased them, snapping at their tails the entire way.

He had lost seven fighters and seven very brave men and women in the fight. The entire casualty list for all twelve transports was just under sixty. The General was stunned at their success and extremely pleased, to say the least. He couldn't believe that twelve transport ships with single-man fighters could turn back a five hundred strong fleet of Dog Warships.

Actually, neither could Saber. But yet they had done it. They had saved Earth and the League.

For the next twenty-four hours, the General had let them all party in their young bodies. As the General said, you all deserve it.

Saber couldn't have agreed more. He had relished every minute of it.

Saber looked around the dim, nursing home room. It was a room he hoped he would never die in. If he died, he wanted it to be in space, fighting for the League and Earth.

Then he laughed, not hard enough to task his old lungs, but enough to relax him a little.

Now he had one task. He had to stay alive until the next mission.

"Anything I can get for you, Captain?" the young soldier asked as he pulled the thin blanket up over Saber's frail body.

"No, thank you, son," Saber said, smiling.

"You did a great job out there, sir," the young man said. "It's an honor knowing you." He snapped to attention, saluted, and then turned for the door.

In a moment the night sounds were shut out and the small nursing home room was silent except for the ticking of the clock.

To the empty room and no one in particular Captain Brian Saber of the Earth Protection League said, "Thank you," very softly. "The honor was all mine."

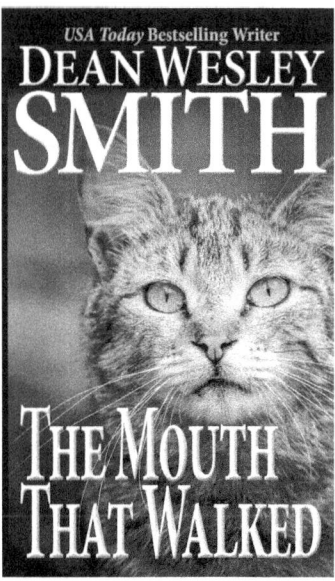

Dean Wesley Smith

USA Today Bestselling Writer

NEVER FORGET
TO SAY GOODBYE.

TUMBLING
DOWN THE NIGHTTIME

Ed lay in his nursing home bed, his sheets wet, the nurses running late in their nightly routine of cleaning him up. He hated the place. He had lived a long and wonderful life and the waiting to die just seemed like too much for him to have to put up with.

But then one night he got a very special visitor from his past, a visitor who had forgotten to say goodbye all those decades before.

TUMBLING DOWN THE NIGHTTIME

ONE

NIGHTLY ROUTINE:

Between one and one-fifteen, the nurse, an over-busted, over-thighed woman with bottle thick glasses would rudely flip on the overhead light, pull back his covers and check to see if the sheets were wet.

They usually were. A source of continued embarrassment. More so with the presence of the almost-always-young, almost-always-pretty aide.

The routine went on.

Without a smile, the nurse would say, "Ed, I'm going to change your bed now and clean you up. All right?" With the help of the aide she'd grab him under the arm and butt and roll him to one side. God, that hurt. Their rough, always-clean hands were sandpaper against his thin, aged skin.

They never asked him to help. He always groaned. What more was there for him to say. Some nights he would try to remember being young, of being with Rebecca, of running and playing baseball. Anything but the routine. But it very seldom took him from the reality. So he just groaned.

In answer to his groan, the nurse would say, "Ed, I've got to change your sheets. It will just take a minute. All right?"

As if he had a choice.

The routine went on.

They'd pull up the sheets from the hall side of the bed while he lay with his back to them, bare ass exposed to God and anyone who chose to walk down the hall at that moment. Then she'd take a wet cloth, always cold, and clean him. Some night he wished the nurse would use a warm cloth.

She never did.

The routine went on.

The two of them would grab him again, roll him back over on the clean sheet side, pull up the rest of the old sheet, and finish putting down the new one. Then, with their sandpaper hands they'd roll him onto his back, pull the sheet loosely over him and flip off the light on the way out, leaving him bruised, battered and exhausted from the battle.

End of routine.

He glanced at his glow-in-the-dark clock. One a.m. The nurse and the aide would be in any moment. He focused his mind on Rebecca, her dark eyes and jet-black hair. They had been lovers for years until finally she had left him, without warning or reason. But those years with her had been his best and they were now the years he focused on when trying to escape the routine.

An intense white flash brought the room into sharp focus before he could snap his eyes shut. It surprised him and he jumped. For a brief moment he thought it

might have been the nurse and the over-head fluorescent bulb had just exploded.

But instead of the nurse's voice or footsteps, a loud crash filled the room. The building groaned. His bed shook. The picture of Maggie, his dead wife, rattled on the night stand. He could hear glass shattering from somewhere down the hall.

Then it ended.

Another new sound. He opened his eyes as shouting came from down the hall. It sounded like he was suddenly in a hospital and someone was trying to die.

The hall lights flickered, then went out. A dull engine sound came from the back of the building and the lights came back on, not quite as bright. Probably the standby generator. He wondered what could have happened to cause the power to go out.

Next he heard doors slam, a woman sob, "Oh, no," and footsteps running. It all ended with one final door slam.

TWO

BUZZERS EXPLODED in the nurse's station like horses from a starting gate as residents, disturbed by the noise, rang for the hired help. That was a sound he always tried, and failed, to put to the back of his mind. The buzzing sound was part of nursing home routine he heard every day. Every hour. A sound that annoyed him, grated at his nerves, and made him angry. He never understood that since he was here to die, why he couldn't do it without the metallic sound of others doing the same thing.

He quickly checked the darkened room. His roommate, Mel, still slept, snoring like he always did. Mel could sleep through anything. Everything else seemed to be in its place. The clock said three minutes after one a.m. He strained to listen for any sound as the clock's ticking got louder and louder until it fought to cover the sounds of the buzzers.

Mel's snoring kept time with the clock. He always slept soundly, dreaming dreams of the war he'd fought in years earlier. His dreams continued through his waking hours and he talked of nothing else. WWII...the Big One. Mel yearned for the time when dying seemed glorious and purposeful instead of boring and without pride. Someday, in a dream, Mel would catch a bullet while leading his platoon and die in his sleep. For him it would then be worthwhile.

The nurse and the aide would change Mel's sheets and roll in a new roommate so Ed would have company. Then he and his new roommate would race to see who would die first.

It had happened twice before. Ed had lost the race both times.

But tonight they were racing on a new track.

Over the buzzers, the ticking of the clock and Mel's battle snores, Ed could hear Mrs. Reeges, two doors down, ring for the nurse. He could tell her buzz because it sounded higher, as if something was slightly broken with it. She always rang around one in the morning. She needed her fix of pills. Sometimes she rang before the nurse attacked him. Sometimes during. Once in a while after. She stayed in her routine now and rang for the nurse, mixing her useless annoyance with that of others.

Mel continued his snoring, successfully dodging bullets, the clock kept its ticking, and a moment later, Mrs. Reeges

rang again. No one answered any of the rings. No movement in the halls at all.

Mrs. Reeges rang again.

Then again.

Where the hell was the damn nurse?

Ed thought about the large woman who changed his bed five nights a week. He knew through the grapevine that she had two kids and a husband who worked swing shift at the plywood plant. She didn't much give a shit about any of the residents. To her they were just like the rough lumber her husband tossed around. The two aides who were the only other employees who worked the night shift were both students and both newly married. They cared even less. It had been lucky nothing much ever happened on graveyard shift. Except people dying. The nurse and the aides never had any trouble with that.

Mrs. Reeges let out a yell.

"Nurse!"

Ed knew she would yell eventually. Others were starting to. Mrs. Reeges would panic and follow their lead.

"Nurse!" Her voice, weak and raspy, barely carried over the rhythmic duo of Mel and the clock.

"Nurse...please?"

All the yelling and buzzing was becoming damn annoying. He could imagine the nurse's station echoing, empty, its colored metal folders in stacked slots with name tags below each. Last week he had noticed that every name tag had a small white tab on the right side to ease in the tags removal when the owner died. That's how it was around here.

Tonight no workers answered the grating sound of the buzzers. No one rushed in to change his sheets. No one would remove his tag when he died. Not even the white tab would help at the moment.

Something major had happened out in the street, or against the side of the building, to make all three employees leave?

Mrs. Reeges rang again, then yelled, "Nurse!"

She had now combined the ring and the yell. She sounded desperate. His sheets felt cold and downright uncomfortable.

Damn it all. "Nurse!" he yelled. His voice sounded weak and hollow. Mel snorted in time with the clock.

Mrs. Reeges rang again. She didn't yell. Maybe she figured that he would do all the yelling. She would do the ringing and he the yelling. Now they were a team of sorts.

"Nurse!" he yelled again, this time his voice carrying more authority. He waited, breathing shallow to hear the answer. He could almost hear Mrs. Reeges waiting, breathing shallow.

She rang again. He yelled with authority. They waited. He could hear over the buzzing, some movement from other residents. No help.

No amount of authority in his yell would bring help. The workers weren't coming back for a while. He was sure of that. He could feel it in the silence over the buzzing and the snoring and the ticking.

Mrs. Reeges rang. She expected him to yell. There was no point.

A minute later, she rang again and yelled, taking up his part of the team. He turned his head from the door toward the curtain over the patio door and the faint light coming from outside.

THREE

"HELLO, ED," a soft voice said and a shadowy shape stepped toward the bed. "Do you need something I can get for you?"

He jerked on the wet sheet like a fish out of water and for a moment he thought

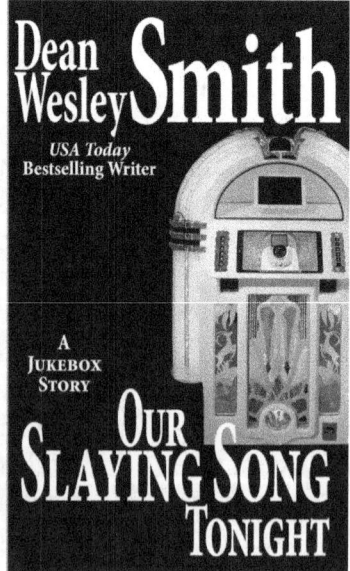

his heart was going to pound right out of his chest. The shadow outlined against the curtains moved closer to the bed as he fought to catch his breath.

"I'm sorry," a woman's voice said. "I didn't mean to startle you."

"But you sure as hell did," Ed managed to choke out while taking deep breaths. "How'd you get in here?"

She laughed softly and Ed's stomach twisted. He knew that laugh. But it couldn't be.

"How about turning on a light so I can see who's giving me a heart attack." He pointed to the lamp on the nightstand beside the bed. The shadow moved to the lamp and with a click lit the room with soft yellow light.

Down the hall the buzzers and the yelling for the nurses continued. Mel kept snoring and life beyond the circle of the lamp light kept on. Ed blinked a few times and then looked up into a face he hadn't seen in forty years, a face that every night he dreamed about, a face that couldn't be. "Rebecca...?"

"Hi, Ed," she said, putting her hand on his arm and her cool touch sent shivers through him. "It's good to see you again."

All he could do was stare. She was still just as young as he remembered her. Her black eyes sparkled in the lamp light and her long black hair shined. She had on a short black leather coat and Levis. And she was more beautiful than he remembered.

He wanted to run, but his body wouldn't move. He wanted to scream, but he knew it would do no good mixed with the calls and buzzers of the others. He wanted to reach out and hug her as he had done forty years ago, but fear held him back.

"Can I sit for a moment?" She pointed to his wheelchair and he somehow managed to nod.

He watched her, trying desperately to clear his mind, as she pulled the chair over beside the bed and sat in it, again putting her cool hand on his arm. He shook his head and laughed. "I'm dreaming aren't I? Or I'm dead and you've

come to take me to heaven. That's it. I'm dead." Somehow that thought comforted him and he managed a deep breath. If he was dead, why couldn't he move? Why couldn't he climb out of bed and go down to the nurse's station and pull his white tag, so everyone would know?

She laughed and again the memories of all those wonderful nights of laughter with her flooded over him as if they had happened yesterday.

"You're not dreaming and you're still very much alive."

Ed sighed. "A guy can always hope."

She squeezed his arm and laughed at his poor joke, but this time he could tell her laugh was not sincere.

"So," he said while rolling the best he could to face her, "after all these years, why are you here? Better yet, why did you leave me in the first place?" And as he talked he noticed that there were absolutely no wrinkles at all in her face or around her eyes. She looked twenty-five years old. "And an even more important question, what's the name of your plastic surgeon?"

She smiled. "To answer your questions one at a time, first I'm here because I wanted to see an old friend and maybe see if I can help you a little."

He didn't say anything. There was no way this could be his Rebecca. She was too young. The real Rebecca would have been eighty-one, two years younger than he was. This must be her granddaughter. But why would her granddaughter pretend to be Rebecca?

"Second," she said, "I left you because I had to. If I had stayed you would have noticed that I wasn't aging and you were."

She held up her hand to stop his comment. "Remember how, that last year we were together, people were commenting on how young I looked? Remember how old Charlie the bartender even said I looked like your daughter? I never changed, did I? In all the years we were together, did I age at all?"

He fought his memory, but he knew she was right. It just hadn't seemed important at the time. It had seemed more like a bonus to him. Not important enough for her to leave him. So what if she looked younger than he did?

"Go on," he said. "Not that I believe any of this, but do please tell me how you stayed so young. He swept his arm in the general direction of the room around them and then at his almost useless body. "I would love to know your secret."

She held his arm firmly and looked him directly in the eye. "I'm what you would call a vampire. I was over three hundred years old when we met. My four hundredth birthday was two months ago."

He stared into her dark eyes, wanting to believe her, and almost, for a short second, he did. Then he fully realized what she had said and the laughter overcame him, slowly building in his stomach and finally erupting in such force that it hurt. Tears filled his eyes and he could feel that he was wetting himself again, the familiar warm feeling mixing with the cold, damp sheets.

She sat up straight in the wheelchair and it rolled an inch or so back from the bed, but she never let go of his arm and the serious expression on her face never changed. After a minute or so he finally stopped laughing and worked at catching his breath.

Mel snorted and rolled over. Down the hall the buzzers and the yelling continued.

"I suppose," he said, between gulps of air, "that you are responsible for the nurse and aides leaving."

She nodded. "It was necessary. I just helped a car go out of control. It hit a power pole and plowed into the side of the building. The driver and three passengers were all drunk, but no one was seriously hurt. The nurse should be returning shortly, as soon as the police arrive, so we don't have much time."

He almost started to laugh again, but the cold sheets under his butt and her stern expression stopped him. "You're serious, aren't you?"

She nodded.

"Okay," he said, lifting himself as best he could with his arms and turning so that he could completely face her. "Assuming that I believe you are a vampire, which I don't, why would you come here to see me now after all these years? You want my thin old blood?"

She looked almost hurt at his sick joke. "Think back," she said. "Did you ever see me in the full light of a summer day?"

"You worked days," he said, but that sounded weak even to him.

"No, I usually slept days. Not that the old myth about sunlight killing us is right. It's not. But direct sunlight is very uncomfortable to me, so I have always preferred nights. All vampires do, thus come the myths. And we haven't killed for blood for centuries."

"That's good to know," he said. "Okay, Rebecca was always a night owl, I will grant you that. But that doesn't make you her. Tell me something about her that only I would know." He smiled at her, figuring he had her. But she smiled back, let go of his arm and stood. In a flash she had unzipped her Levis and pulled them down enough to expose white lace panties. Facing the lamp she pulled the panties down to the top of her black pubic hair and there was the birthmark.

Rebecca's birthmark.

He glanced up into her serious eyes and then back at the apple-shaped birthmark. An apple with what looked to be a bite taken out of it. A very distinctive, one-of-a-kind birthmark.

Three Seeders Universe Novels
Available at your favorite booksellers.

"You always used to call it the 'apple of your eye' because you liked to look at it so much." She laughed, again a sincere, deep laugh. "In fact, the last few years you called it an appetizer because it always came right before the main course."

The room was spinning and he closed his eyes to force it to stop. The clock kept ticking and Mel kept snoring. Down the hall the buzzers were still going strong. He must be having a nightmare. He would wake up, open his eyes, and the nightly routine would be about to start. It would only be one a.m. and the nurse would be coming to change his sheets.

He would laugh at the nightmare and tell Mel about it tomorrow morning, birthmark and all. Rebecca was a vampire who had come back to visit him. That would get old Mel laughing for sure.

He opened his eyes. The buzzing continued and the clock said fifteen minutes after one a.m. Rebecca was again sitting in his wheelchair, her cold hand on his arm.

For the longest time he did nothing but stare into her eyes.

The clock ticked. Mel snored. Buzzers buzzed. And he looked into her eyes.

Finally he said, "It really is you, isn't it?"

She had the grace to only nod.

He nodded with her, suddenly more tired than he had felt in years. "So why come back to me now, after forty years?"

She looked away, her gaze moving in jerks around the room. Finally her gaze stopped on the picture of his wife, Maggie, that rested on his nightstand. Maggie had been dead for seven years. They had met and married three years after Rebecca had left him. It had been a good marriage, but nothing more.

"I think I would have liked her," she said, nodding at the picture.

"You can tell that from a picture? Another special power?"

She half laughed. "No, I'm afraid not. I don't think you ever realized how much I loved you. For most of the past forty years I have kept track of you, watched your life, always from a distance."

"You did?" He stared at her while she continued to stare at the picture of Maggie.

She nodded. "I even managed to meet and talk to Maggie a number of times when you weren't around. Twice, as a matter of fact, in the grocery store line. She seemed to be a very nice person and I was happy for you. It made me very sad when she died."

He glanced at the picture of Maggie and then back at Rebecca, his first and only true love. "I loved her, but never as much as I loved you."

Rebecca turned to face him. "I know," she said. Her grip was firm on his arm and he placed his other hand over hers.

They stayed that way, in silence, as Mel snored, buzzers called for attention, and the clock ticked the night away.

After a short time a door slammed down the hall and the sounds of talking drifted over the commotion.

"I don't have much time," she said. "The nurse will be coming soon."

"So come back tomorrow night. We can talk about old times."

She shook her head no. "I'm moving on. I have a husband and he was transferred back east to Chicago. We're leaving tomorrow."

"Is he a vampire, too?"

"No," she said softly.

"So you will one day leave him too?"

She looked away, back at Maggie's picture. "Everyone leaves someone sometime. It's the way of the world."

He glanced at the picture of Maggie and then back at Rebecca. "I knew why Maggie left me. She even said good-bye. I always wondered why you did not."

"I know. That's one of the reasons I'm here tonight."

"What's his name?"

"Craig. His name is Craig."

"And you love him?"

She nodded. "Yes, I think I do. But I also still love you." She looked him directly in the eyes and he knew, without a doubt that she was telling the truth.

They continued to stare at each other. She was still so beautiful, so young and he was so old, so crippled. It didn't seem fair to him that it had turned out this way.

When the buzzers all shut off at once he knew the time was short. He could feel Rebecca starting to pull away. "You said you might be able to help me? What did you mean by that?"

Rebecca glanced at Maggie's picture again and then back into his eyes.

"Can you make me young again? Make me into someone like you? A vampire?"

She shook her head no. "It doesn't work that way. But I can help you out of this."

She nodded at the room and it took him a moment staring into her serious expression to completely understand. "You could do that?"

She nodded. "If it's what you want."

He laughed a light, half-hearted laugh. "It's been what I have wanted since my legs quit working and I ended up in this damn room. Every night I hope, and even pray, that I will die so I won't have to wake up in a wet bed, or have some nurse's aide lift me onto the toilet in the morning. Getting out of here has been my strongest wish for five years."

She didn't say a word and again, after a short moment of looking at her, he asked, "You're serious, aren't you?"

She nodded.

He closed his eyes and listened to the sounds of the night. The sirens outside, of the police coming to the wreck, the muffled talking from the nurse and aides drifting down the hall, Mel's snoring, and the continuous ticking of the clock.

How many nights had he wished for this very thing?

How many thousand nights had he wished he could see Rebecca again?

How many thousand nights had he wished he would just die so he could escape this old, useless body he found himself trapped in?

How many nights?

And now he had both of his wishes all wrapped up together like a sick joke.

He opened his eyes and gazed into her concerned face. "You know, you are as beautiful as ever."

She half smiled and squeezed his arm as the nurse and aides went into the room across the hall. He would be next on their rounds.

"Thanks for the offer. But I think I will pass. I'd just like to remember you like this."

This time her smile filled her face and the relief was obvious. "I still love you," she said as she leaned forward and kissed his cheek.

"And I love you."

She stood and looked at him for a short moment. Then she moved toward the window.

"Wait!"

She turned, one hand on the drapes.

"Say good-bye this time."

She nodded. "Good-bye, Ed."

"Now that wasn't so hard was it? And when the time comes promise me you will say that to Craig."

She stared at him for what seemed like a long, long time. Then she smiled. "I promise."

"Good," he said.

"I love you." She pulled the curtains back and disappeared into the black night.

"I love you, too," he said to the swaying curtains.

A moment later the florescent overhead light snapped on and the nurse, an over-busted, over-thighed woman with bottle thick glasses stepped into the room. "Sorry we're late, Ed," she said. "There was an accident outside, so it's been a long night."

"No, actually," he said, still staring at the curtains, "it's been a short life."

The nurse looked at him oddly for a moment, then said, "Let's check to see if these sheets are wet."

And the routine started again.

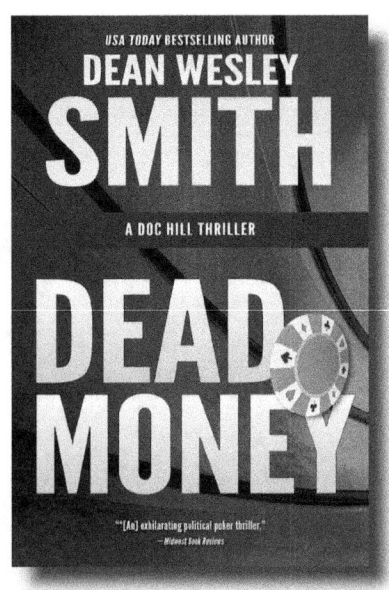

Available at Your Favorite Bookstore

Dean Wesley Smith
USA Today Bestselling Writer

IN SEARCH OF
THE PERFECT
ORGASM
(OR HOW DOING IT WITH A GIANT LIZARD CAN BE FUN)

Ask what happens when the powerful lust of a teenager gets on a collision course with aliens fighting an ancient Japanese monster. Go ahead: Ask.

USA Today bestselling writer Dean Wesley Smith bets you don't come up with this answer.

IN SEARCH OF THE PERFECT ORGASM (Or How Doing It With A Giant Lizard Can Be Fun)

INTRODUCTION

I seldom feel the need to do an introduction to a short story, especially one as short as this story. But this story has played a fun and important part in my writing career over the years.

Yes, this story.

Honest.

It all started in a time far, far away.

Wonderful writer and sometimes editor, Esther M. Friesner, had been hired by Martin H. Greenberg to edit an anthology for Daw Books called Alien Pregnant by Elvis.

Esther called me (long, long, long before the days of e-mail) and asked if I would like to write a story for the crazy idea. The fact that she thought of me for such a strange anthology tells you what my reputation was like back then.

I said to Esther, "Sure, who wouldn't want to write for such a fun idea?"

And then I went and wrote this goofy story. I showed it to Kris (almost said my wife, but I wrote this story before Kristine Kathryn Rusch and I were married) and she laughed, shook her head, and luckily didn't leave me for daring to write something like this.

Esther loved the story and somehow she got the powers-that-be in publishing both at Tekno Books and Daw Books to let the story stay in the book, and off we went into publishing land.

A year later or so, the book came out. I hadn't seen a copy yet and I had forgotten I even had a story in the book, to be honest.

One fine evening, Kris and I were sitting in our new home (we were married by this point and I'm fairly certain it had nothing to do with this story). We were watching the Science Fiction Channel. (Long before it was called the SciFi Channel.)

At that time, the channel was brand new and it had a weekly science fiction news program about movies, books, comics, and so on, hosted by someone I am too lazy to go look up.

The show for the week was about finished when suddenly the host started talking with one of his assistants, a beautiful model-like woman. He held a book in his hand and kept waving it around like he was going to hit himself with it.

He asked her, "Have you read this story by Dean Wesley Smith yet in this Esther M. Friesner anthology?"

She said no as he waved the book around even more excitedly in the air.

(Kris started laughing. I was falling off the couch. Now I remembered the story.)

The host went on. "It's about searching for the perfect orgasm. At least that's what the title says."

(I fell off the couch.)

"I really got to read that," she said, reaching for the book.

"No, me first," he said, or something like that, and they pretended to fight over the book as the show ended. (I honestly have no memory of how they ended the bit because I was on the floor laughing.)

Flash forward to present, more years than I want to think about…

Over the years this crazy little story has become one of my most reprinted short stories. It seems that everyone wants to read about searching for the perfect orgasm.

So read on.

I hope you enjoy the story as much as I enjoyed writing it and all the crazy things that have happened because of it over the years.

(Actually, I have no memory of writing it, but I've sure enjoyed having written it.)

ONE

WHEN THE ALIEN ray gun zapped Godzilla, it did more than just jab at the old cliché, it burnt a few people, too. This is the story of one of those people: Little

Sally Ann Gibson, age eighteen, size 36D, ray-gun victim.

TWO

COUNTDOWN:
ONE HOUR BEFORE
GODZILLA BITES IT.

"Sally. Ann. Gibson."

Sally's mother spaced the words as if they were each a sentence.

"How many times have I told you to wear a bra? You can't go to school looking like that. Now get back upstairs and change into something decent."

"But mom…" Sally banged her hand in frustration on the banister, not really noticing that her anger made her nipples poke through the loose knit of the sweater.

"Do as I say."

Sally's mom put her hands on her hips in the old Superman pose and stared at Sally's chest with disgust.

Sally knew there was no arguing with her mother when she talked like that and stood like that. It made no difference that all the girls in school were going without their bras. It made no difference that she had great tits and liked to show them off. Nope. None of that mattered. Her mom was still living in the stone-age.

Sally trudged slowly back upstairs, pouting, her lower lip extended, wondering what Billy was going to think and if he'd even like her any more. It wasn't until she got to the top of the stairs that she realized she was being stupid. She could just take her bra off when she got to school. Her mom would never know.

And it might even be fun.

COUNTDOWN:
THIRTY MINUTES BEFORE THE
ALIEN RAY GUN
FRIES GODZILLA'S BRAIN
AND OTHER BODY PARTS.

Sally giggled, then squirmed on the car seat as Billy slipped her sweater up over her head. His fingers were cold and as they brushed her skin under her arms they tickled and sent shivers of pleasure all over her body.

"Nice way to start the day," Billy said, his hands rubbing her bra-encased boobs as if he was trying to tune her grandfather's old radio, both knobs at the same time.

Sally glanced nervously around the mostly empty school parking lot. It was still early, so there was time. She turned her back to Billy. "Unhook me, would you?"

"My pleasure," Billy said. His voice squeaked and he was starting to pant. Sally knew what that meant. She'd have to get her sweater back on damn fast or they'd be wrestling out here for hours. Damn. Why had she thought it would be fun to have Billy help?

THREE

COUNTDOWN:
TEN MINUTES UNTIL GODZILLA
GETS TURNED TO A CRISPY
CRITTER BY THE ALIENS WHO
WANT TO SAVE EARTH FOR
SOMETHING BETTER.

"Billy! Stop that!"

Sally pulled Billy's hand out from under her skirt.

Now she was doing the panting.

His face was red.

She had gotten her sweater back on only by promising Billy he could do other "things." She just hadn't expected to enjoy the other "things" so much. She had always been a "good" girl and had never let a boy touch her "there."

She glanced quickly around the still almost empty parking lot. Well, maybe it wouldn't hurt for just another minute.

She let go of Billy's hand and it ducked under her skirt faster than her cat trying to hide from the neighbor's dog.

FOUR

COUNTDOWN:
FIVE MINUTES UNTIL GODZILLA SMOKES AND THE ALIENS LAUGH AND THE WORLD IS PLAGUED WITH A NEW RASH OF JAPANESE HORROR MOVIES.

Sally and Billy were interrupted twice by cars pulling in. But both times, Sally let Billy put his hand back up under her skirt. The last time he had pulled aside her white panties and really touched her. The feeling almost scared her.

Almost.

This time, the intruding car, Carla's blue Volks, pulled in across from them.

Billy quickly pulled his hand out and Sally felt the disappointment, among other things. The excitement of thinking that Carla might guess what they were doing had her breathing hard.

Both of them waved at Carla as if they had been talking about a biology assignment. The minute Carla turned and headed for the school, Sally lifted her butt off the seat, reached up under her skirt, and pulled off her white panties. She held them up for Billy to see.

Billy's eyes were as wide as saucers and he swallowed hard.

"If I don't need a bra," she said, smiling. "I sure don't see why I need these."

She dropped them into her purse as Billy tried to catch his breath.

FIVE

COUNTDOWN:
ONE MINUTE UNTIL GODZILLA GETS STEAMED, DEEP-FAT FRIED, AND SENT TO THE NEXT WORLD BY THE ALIENS WHO AREN'T EVEN FROM THIS WORLD.

Billy's fingers were doing wonderful things under her skirt and Sally didn't really care if anyone drove up or not. She'd let Billy watch out.

She had her eyes closed and her entire body was starting to tremble.

She knew she was going to come any minute.

And she knew it was going to be a lot better than when she wrapped her legs around her teddy bear and squeezed real hard.

Billy's hand moved faster and she moaned.

This time was going to be much better.

SIX

BLAST-OFF:
GODZILLA'S SCALES
REFLECTED PART
OF THE HEAT RAY.
ALIEN GUNNERS CALLED IT A
FLUKE.

Billy's hand was moving like a blender and Sally was half moaning, half shouting. Two seniors laughed and pointed as they walked by the shaking car.

SEVEN

HEADLINE:
ALIEN RAY BOUNCES OFF
GOZILLA, THEN ATMOSPHERE,
HITS CAR IN A HIGH SCHOOL
PARKING LOT IN THE VERY
HEART OF AMERICA.
PRESIDENT THREATENS TO SUE
ALIENS AND JAPANESE.

Sally Ann Gibson's first real orgasm and the alien heat ray hit her at exactly the same instant.

She exploded like a kid's balloon against a cactus.

She blew up like a tomato thrown against a brick wall.

She had an orgasm unparalleled in human existence.

EIGHT

HEADLINE:
GODZILLA LIMPS INTO
OCEAN CARRYING TEN-STORY
BUILDING.
ALIENS HAVE NO COMMENT.

Billy broke his right hand in the orgasmic explosion and ended up having to sell what was left of his car because he couldn't get past the memory. He also had to live with a phobia against parking on dates that limited his future sexual practices and cost him years of counseling.

Little Sally Ann Gibson recovered after two days in the hospital.

The doctors promised her that plastic surgery would help the permanent smile frozen on her face.

She never had the operation.

Available at Your Favorite Bookstore

USA TODAY BESTSELLING AUTHOR

DEAN WESLEY SMITH

STAR RAIN

A SEEDERS UNIVERSE NOVEL

The fight with the genetically engineered aliens seemed impossible. Benny and Gina, both Seeders, stood on the bridge of their massive mother ship knowing they needed miracles to win.

They both knew that if they worked long enough and hard enough, miracles might happen. Centuries worth of work.

A massive scale Seeders Universe story that started in the novel Star Mist *in the last* Smith's Monthly *issue.*

STAR RAIN
A Seeders Universe Novel

For Kris

SECTION ONE
The Fight is Lost

PROLOGUE
(Twenty-seven years before the discovery of the aliens…)

THE LAST THREE years had gone faster than Chairman Evan West had expected. Around him on the command center of the *Rescue One,* the fifteen members of his main crew were all standing ready at their stations on the three levels, all scanning ahead as much as they could.

He knew that through the entire ship the thirty thousand people on board were also watching intently.

West was a tall, thin man with bright green eyes, balding head, and wide shoulders. People said he had a smile that made him a lot of friends and he liked to laugh and have fun.

Lately he hadn't smiled much.

The air was tense in the large room around him, but professional. The large screen that filled the tall wall in front of them only showed the quickly approaching front edge of the small galaxy they were calling Destination. The galaxy had a number, but no one called it by that anymore.

West stood beside his large chairman's chair, watching not only his instruments, but those of his second and third in command at their stations on either side of him.

Nothing.

Just nothing out of the ordinary at all.

They were on a mission to find out what had happened to the *Dreaming Large,* one of the huge Seeder mother ships. It had vanished in the small galaxy they were now approaching.

That had been four years ago, a short time for a Seeder, but a very long time for a major mother ship to vanish completely.

Mother ships were the size of large moons and built to look like a giant bird in flight. A mother ship could hold a few thousand smaller ships and upward of a million or more people. It was from the mother ships that Seeders spread humanity from one galaxy to another, always moving forward.

Chairman West had been a seeder now for three thousand years and had seen many galaxies along the way. And he had helped in birthing more billions of human societies than he wanted to even try to imagine.

He loved his job.

He didn't much like this mission.

His wife and best friend, Tammy, had been on the *Dreaming Large* when it vanished. He missed their nightly routines of telling each other their days through a trans-tunnel link, even when they had been apart for years. He loved her and always had loved her. They had been a team for centuries.

And he missed her now more than he wanted to ever admit.

Their plan had been for him to finish up the last part of a seeding mission in the previous galaxy and then his ship and a dozen other front-line ships with him would catch up with the *Dreaming Large.* He liked working the front edge of the seeding as he always did after the terraforming was finished.

He had worried for the three years it took them at full trans-tunnel speed to get here and he had missed Tammy every moment of it. He had no idea what they were going to find. No one had an idea, even though the speculation was rampart.

How could a major Seeder mother ship simply vanish?

Without a word of notice, the two chairmen who jointly ran the mother ship had stopped reporting in to Chairman Ray.

When that had happened, Chairman Ray had contacted him and the idea of *Rescue One* was born.

There were twenty-two mother ships now, built over centuries, with more being built all the time. The *Dreaming Large* was the first to vanish.

Tammy had been one of the head botanists on *Dreaming Large.* She had loved her job, just as he loved his.

The *Rescue One* had been built especially for this mission.

Unlike most Seeders' ships, the *Rescue One* had a full military contingent and four warships on board, commanded by West's best friend, Ben Cline. Seeders, by their very mission and scouting ahead, never had much need for military until some of the growing new human cultures hit their early space age stage. So to even put together a military fleet, Cline had scrounged through some more advanced human cultures recently seeded for ships and enough new Seeders to man the ships.

It had taken Cline as long to put his force together as it had to build the *Rescue One*.

The *Rescue One* had been built in preparation for almost anything they might find. It also had in its huge hangar twenty of the Seeders' fastest scout ships, all crewed with upward of twenty thousand people each and ready to go.

And it had room, if necessary, for a hundred thousand survivors, a fraction of the humans who had been on the *Dreaming Large* when it vanished.

Now, finally, after the year of building and three years of travel at the fastest trans-tunnel speeds any Seeder ship could go, they were almost there.

"Anything?" West asked, breaking the silence on the large command center and glancing around the three levels at his first shift crew.

All of them shook their heads.

"Full stop at scouting distance from the edge of Destination," he ordered.

"We'll be at full stop in one minute," Korgan said.

Korgan was his second in command and had been chairman of his own scout ship before volunteering to go on this mission. He had family, a son and a daughter, on the *Dreaming Large*.

In fact, a good third of the crew of the *Rescue One* had family or some personal connection to crew on the *Dreaming Large*.

That made this crew very, very motivated to find the lost mother ship.

"Dropping out of trans-warp now," Korgan said, his voice seeming to almost echo in the silence of the large bridge.

"Full scans," West said.

Then he motioned to Korgan to have the crews of the scout ships stand ready and be scanning as well.

West moved over and stood beside his command chair. He couldn't make himself sit in the chair until they knew what had happened to *Dreaming Large.* But from where he stood, he could see all the data streaming in.

Destination was a small spiral galaxy on the scheme of things, with about 80 billion stars of all standard sizes. It showed no unusual areas at all.

And not a sign of the *Dreaming Large.*

Nothing.

The huge mother ship had just vanished.

West left his chairman's chair after a few minutes and walked slowly around to all the stations on his bridge, not so much for information, but to give everyone some time and let himself relax a little.

He had been preparing for this moment for four years. Rushing anything now might lead to even more problems.

Finally, after the longest half hour he had ever spent in the command center, he broke the intense silence.

"Let's have some reports," he said. "So everyone can be together on this. And broadcast these reports to the entire ship please."

Korgan nodded for West to go ahead.

"Anything unusual at all about Destination?"

Three stations reported in that there was nothing unusual. Then Korgan added. "What we are reading matches exactly the last reports of the scout ships two hundred years before the *Dreaming Large* arrived here."

West nodded. "Any signs of alien or human habitation?"

Six reports came in quickly, one after another, cutting the small galaxy down into six quadrants, just as it would have been seeded.

Nothing.

No alien life, no human life, no remains of any ship anywhere.

As with most galaxies, this one was empty. And if it had an alien race at any level anywhere in the galaxy, the entire galaxy would have just been left alone and the *Dreaming Large* would have gone on to the next empty galaxy.

Not one sign that the *Dreaming Large* had even started terraforming the Goldilocks zone planets around yellow stars. Whatever had happened, it had happened before the *Dreaming Large* entered Destination.

"More information as we have it," West said, signaling to Korgan to cut the communication to the entire ship.

West did one more walk around the bridge, looking at details on a few reports, but finding nothing different at all.

Finally, he went down to stand near his station.

"*Rescue One,*" he said, "please put on the screen a two-dimensional representation of the galaxies closest to Destination. Limit the galaxies to a one-year travel time for the *Dreaming Large* from this point."

Thirty-one galaxies came up, represented as dots. There were a couple clusters and ten galaxies seemed to have formed a group. Over the last three years he had stared at this very map more than he wanted to admit.

But he knew that the *Dreaming Large* would not have gone to any of those other galaxies without reporting in. And with Destination being an empty galaxy, perfect for seeding, there would have been no reason to move on.

This was exactly what he had feared. What Chairman Ray had also feared.

"Now, *Rescue One*," West said to his ship, "please add into the scanning equipment the ability to see pockets of empty space."

Everyone on the bridge crew just stopped and looked at him like he had lost a marble or two.

Almost no one had heard of empty space. He hadn't either until this mission started.

West had been briefed by Chairman Ray and his wife, Chairman Tacita, on the very reality of empty space, or void space as it was sometimes called.

Basically, empty space was a very small bubble in space, often not more than the size of a standard solar system, where space was completely empty and time and the rules of physics did not apply for some reason inside it.

Over the centuries, Seeder ships had just vanished when they ran into a bubble of empty space.

And they would often emerge thousands, if not hundreds of thousands of years later having only spent less than a shipboard few hours in empty space.

Chairman Ray had warned West that if there were no logical reasons for *Star Fall* to have vanished, no signs of any debris, or any human survivors, then West was to look for empty space pockets.

The scientists on some of the more advanced Seeder ships had developed a program to show complete emptiness, something normal space did not have.

It had taken the scientists three years of frantic work to finally develop and test the long-range scanning program.

And if this worked, every Seeder ship would get the program as an update and hopefully no more ships would be lost to centuries in an empty space bubble.

For the year that the scanning program had been uploaded to *Rescue One*, the scientists had continued to make adjustments and sent them along. West had told no one about any of it.

"Loaded," *Rescue One* said.

"Display on the screen as dots the empty space areas within four galaxies radius of this location," West said.

Then red dots appeared. Only about eight total in that much space, but one was seemingly right where they were.

They were within brushing distance of the edge of an empty space bubble.

"Shit!' West said. "Back us away from the edge of that thing to a distance of two light years."

West couldn't believe that they had almost vanished right into empty space as well.

That had been far, far too close.

"We're back away from it," Korgan reported a few long moments later. "What exactly is empty space?"

"That's where the *Dreaming Large* is trapped," West said.

The big mother ship had to be right here very close to them, only stuck in a bubble of no time and space. And the mother ship might not emerge for a hundred thousand years.

All West could see in his mind was the smiling face of his wife.

Somehow, they had to rescue the big ship, even though, more than likely, no one on the big ship even knew anything was wrong yet.

But he and *Rescue One* and its crew had to pull off the impossible and get *Dreaming Large* out of there.

Somehow.

***

Over the next five years, the *Rescue One* went from a military-based rescue operation to a full-fledged science ship. West had remained as chairman on request, a request that Chairman Ray had gladly granted.

And Chairman Ray had put West in charge of the overall mission. All ships' chairmen in the area reported to him.

Entire parts of *Rescue One* were being reconfigured into research labs to study the empty space bubble holding the *Dreaming Large* mother ship.

Admiral Cline had taken all his military ships and headed back to help out at the last seeded galaxy with upcoming wars between developing human planets.

The fleet of scout ships they had brought with them all scattered out to do what they do, scout ahead, map galaxies and spot trouble galaxies that had the occasional growing alien race.

Almost every day another science ship arrived at *Rescue One* and took a location either in space near *Rescue One* or on one of the large decks where the military ships and scout ships had once been housed.

Almost fifty smaller science ships had now surrounded the small bubble of empty space, studying it, trying to see inside it.

Every Seeder's ship now had the scanning ability to see and avoid empty space bubbles, something that West had no doubt would save ships from losing thousands and thousands of years.

Now they just had to figure out a way to get the *Dreaming Large* out of there in under a few thousand years.

Every day Chairman West had a meeting with the four top science advisors to get reports on any progress. They usually met for breakfast in his own kitchen in his apartment, taking turns cooking and cleaning and talking about the problem.

All four were chairmen of their own major science ships.

It was right before one meeting that West came up with an idea. He had been sitting at his kitchen counter, staring at a surface rendering of the patterns on the border of the empty space and he suddenly saw it a different way.

They had been working to find a way to shield themselves from the effects of the empty space, go in and shield *Dreaming Large* as well. What would happen if they just drained the empty space out into normal space?

Or better yet, filled empty space with normal space.

In essence, they needed to pop the bubble, leaving the *Dreaming Large* surprised at all the company it suddenly had around it.

The four scientists loved that idea and after the meeting, West contacted Chairman Ray and told him about it to get scientists in numbers of galaxies working on the problem as well.

It took seven more years to find the solution.

Seven very long and frustrating years.

Now West stood in the command center of the *Rescue One* yet again, sixteen years after he had agreed to join this project, ready to try to finally release *Dreaming Large*.

As everyone had been warned, no one on *Dreaming Large* would even realize they had been in trouble. As far as those on board the giant mother ship knew, only a few seconds had transpired since they entered empty space and their trans-tunnel drives had suddenly shut down.

If what *Rescue One* and all the other ships were about to do worked, the hundreds and hundreds of ships that now swarmed the area would suddenly just appear to those on *Dreaming Large*.

If it worked.

And if the forces didn't pull *Dreaming Large* apart.

Chairman Ray and others had said that the giant mother ships were designed to withstand plowing into planets and going right on through. Ray wasn't worried about that at all.

But West was.

They had calculated the trajectory where *Dreaming Large* had entered the empty space bubble and cleared every ship out of the way where it would be headed.

What they were going to try to do was in essence take the pressure of empty space away by opening not just one, but thousands of holes in it all at once. Just as firefighters did to a burning structure under pressure. They opened many outlets instead of just one.

The scientists a few years back had determined exactly what strange gravitational force was holding empty space together like a bubble, allowing a ship to enter and leave, yet holding the space together.

And once they had determined that force, they knew how to puncture the force to not so much let empty space out, but to let regular space and time flood in.

The entire bubble should, the scientists had told West, just vanish as if it had never existed.

West could only hope.

"Report status," West said to all the ships around the bubble ready to send a hundred probes each to open up holes.

A moment later Korgan looked up at him and nodded. "All eighty ships report green, Chairman."

West nodded, staring at the big screen in front of him showing nothing but empty space.

"Mission go," West said.

West knew that once he said that, a computer program from *Rescue One* would launch all probes at the exact same moment from all ships.

West had been told that the probes would have a small charge when they hit the membrane, so it would look like eight thousand tiny lights flashing at the same time in a sphere shape in open space.

"Five seconds," Korgan said.

Intense, heavy silence filled the bridge of the ship.

West had no doubt not one word was being said anywhere in the large fleet of ships surrounding the empty space bubble.

West could not for a second take his gaze away from the massive screen in front of him.

Suddenly, there was a white flash of light from what looked like the surface of a sphere.

Then a moment later, the massive mother ship *Dreaming Large* appeared.

Cheering erupted around the bridge.

West just stood there grinning, staring at the screen, knowing that finally, after sixteen years, he would finally get to see his wife's face again. And maybe a little later actually hug her and kiss her.

After a moment, Korgan, a smile almost splitting his face, turned to West. "I have the two chairmen of the *Dreaming Large* asking just what the hell is going on."

West just smiled right back at Korgan. "Tell them to contact Chairman Ray and let him explain."

Then, for seemingly the first time in sixteen years, he went and sat down in his chairman's chair.

And then on a private channel he said to *Rescue One*, "Please contact my wife on *Dreaming Large* and put her through to my personal screen here."

"I will be glad to, Chairman," *Rescue One* said.

"Thank you," he said.

And then, for the first time in sixteen years, he took a deep breath and relaxed.

One

(Sixty-three years after the rescue of the *Dreaming Large*)

CHAIRMAN BENNY SLADE stood beside Gina Helm, his co-chairman of the Seeder mother ship *Star Rain,* in their massive command center, watching the newest reports come in on the big wall-sized screen from their sector of space.

Beside them their molded joint command chair dominated the large room, but neither of them felt like sitting in it at the moment.

There were twenty others at stations in the command center behind them and not a person was saying a word. The room was the size of a banquet room and three levels, with one wall filled with a massive screen.

Benny had on his normal jeans and dress shirt with the sleeves rolled up. He worked out and ran every day and kept his dark hair military short. He loved this job more than anything he could have ever imagined. But sometimes, on days like today, he would rather be doing just about anything else.

Gina was as tall as his six-foot height, had black hair, and was in as good shape physically as he was. She had on a long-sleeve white blouse, jeans, and tennis shoes. She always kept her long black hair pulled back and tied.

Benny loved Gina more than he could ever imagine loving another human being, and now, after thirty plus years together, couldn't imagine not having her at his side.

"So, what do you think," Gina asked softly, staring at the last reports flowing over the big screen. Everyone in the command center could see the data and no one was saying a word. Tomb-like silence, never a good thing as far as Benny was concerned.

"We're losing this goddamned fight," Benny said.

Gina only nodded.

As more and more scout ships were put out to find alien galaxies, and as the scout ships found the galaxies, many of them just teeming with alien planets, the more it became clear the impossibility of the fight they faced.

Benny glanced around at their command crew as they worked at their stations, quietly, making sure everything on the massive mother ship was running smoothly and clearly not wanting to acknowledge what Benny had just said.

Their ship, *Star Rain,* was shaped like a large bird gliding through space, but it was larger than most moons and functioned more like a flying city than anything else. And it was all controlled by *Star Rain* and the team in this command center.

And Benny knew that all of the team behind him were basically looking at the same data he and Gina were staring at on the big screen.

And he had no doubt all of them were coming to the same damn conclusion he and Gina were facing.

They were losing.

Every one of the over one million people on the *Star Rain* knew it.

No one was talking about giving up or retreating, but unless a miracle occurred, they were not going to be able to contain the aliens.

But they had no real choice if all human-settled galaxies were going to survive. They had to stop this plague of rat-like aliens somehow.

But damned if any of them knew how.

Gina took his hand and squeezed it. They had been together now ever since he had set up the Empire State Building in his hometown of New York City to house survivors from a planetwide disaster.

She had been a Seeder and assigned to help him. After they had met, he had become a Seeder as well and together they had stayed on his home planet to help in the recovery and rebuilding.

Three long years they worked on the surface, including moving to Portland, one of the new centers of the recovering civilization. That task has seemed impossible as well.

And then one day, seemingly out of the blue, they had been offered this job to be joint chairmen of a massive million-person Seeder mother ship.

It seemed he and Gina had great Seeder genes or some such thing. Benny had never completely understood that and honestly had never gotten around to asking or looking it up. It didn't matter, they took the job and now stood here.

Three mother ships had been sent to investigate an alien culture, only to find out the alien culture was manmade. The aliens, as everyone just called them, looked like rats and were no smarter than rats, actually, and thanks to the stupidity of their creators, the aliens were spreading faster from galaxy to galaxy than could be stopped.

Benny hated rats. He had right from the start in New York.

Now they had been fighting this fight against these alien rats for sixteen years.

And Benny was feeling more frustrated by the day.

"Chairmen Ray and Tacita are asking for you presence on the *Star Mist*," *Star Rain* reported.

Star Rain, their wonderful ship, had an intelligence that was more like their friend to Gina and him than a huge ship. But without *Star Rain,* nothing in this moon-sized ship would work.

Gina laughed. "Wonder if this is more bad news."

Benny smiled at her and then pointed to the big screen. "More bad news? I thought I was the fatalistic one around here."

"Oh, yeah, I forgot," she said, smiling at him and talking in her pretend voice. "Let's go hear the great news they bring that will pull our asses out of this fire and save the day."

"That's better," he said, laughing.

It sure had seemed over the years, since this fight had started, that more bad news had come than good. The aliens had expanded from their first world in three major directions and had been expanding for a couple hundred thousand years now.

The human idiots who designed and genetically built the aliens were an old group who had split away from the Seeders millions of years before. They called themselves The Creators. They believed in being able to create intelligent life from alien structures.

Now they were also fighting against their own creations. No one on a Seeder ship had even talked with them.

And a second ancient fleet of humans calling themselves The Exterminators had followed The Creators and were working now as well to clean up this mess.

So now three fleets of humans were attacking this problem and none of them talking to the other. Benny agreed that at this point, that was for the best.

The idiot Creators had given the aliens only two major drives. First was to have offspring, litters and litters of them.

Now Available
from all your favorite booksellers
in trade paper and electronic editions.

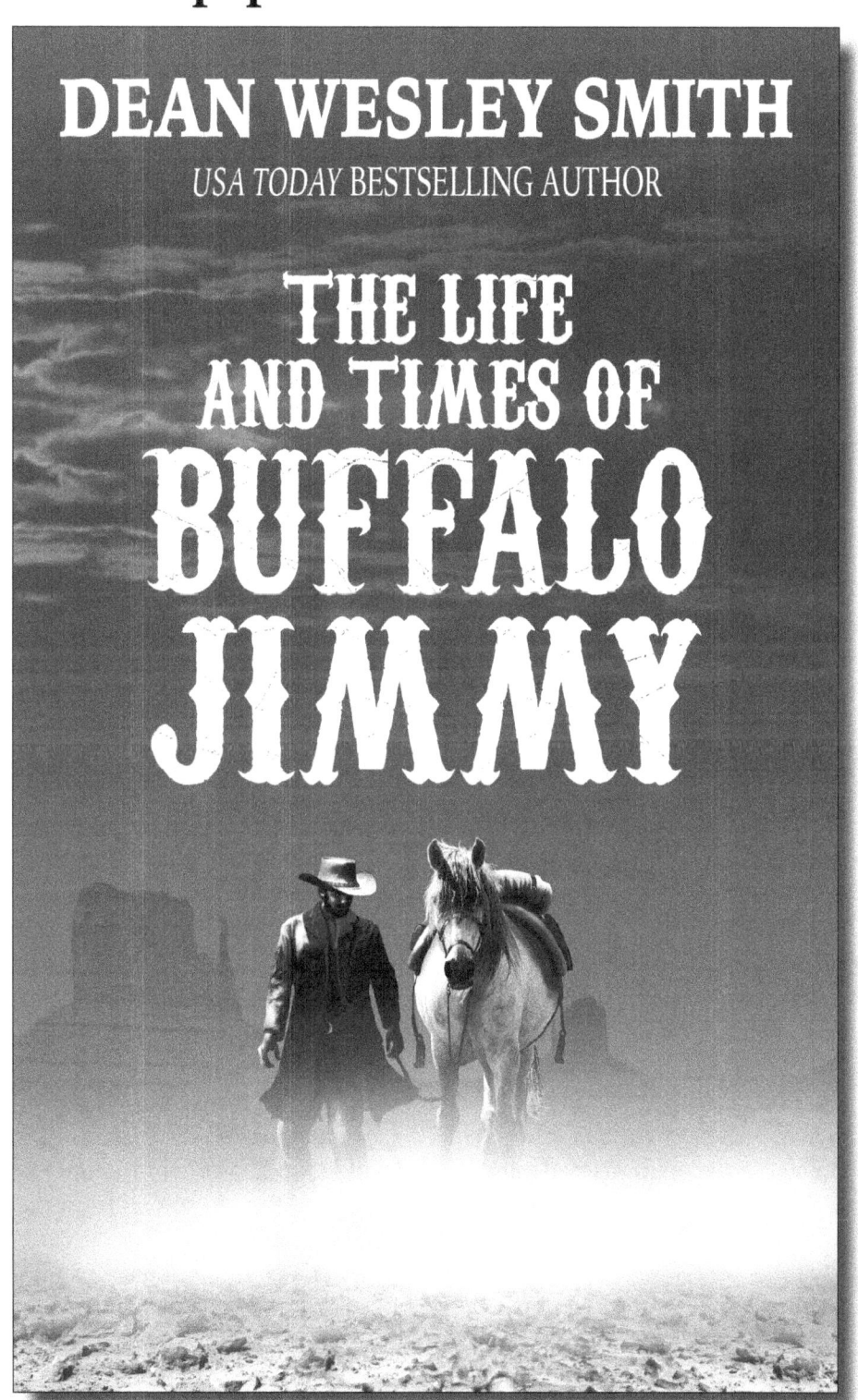

Second designed-in drive was to build trans-tunnel spaceships from a certain pattern and expand to other planets. What a stupid idea. Benny wanted to just meet the Creators and lift them off the ground and shake them and ask them what the hell they were thinking.

The Creators also forgot to program in the aliens simple things like survival and an ability to learn as they went.

In fact, the aliens were almost as dumb as rats in New York. Actually, Benny had seen smarter rats in New York. Thank heavens no one had given the rats in New York the ability to build spaceships.

The more the aliens had been studied over the sixteen years, the more all of the chairmen had come to the conclusion that this race really wasn't intelligent in any real sense of the word. The aliens were just a programmed higher-form rat-like animal and nothing more.

Programmed to breed, expand by building a simple ship, and destroy anything in its way to build more ships.

Benny had a gut sense the destroying part hadn't been programmed in, but was just part of the nature of the creatures.

Rats.

He flat hated rats.

What was amazing is that the aliens didn't even realize they were in a war with their creators. Awareness and communication between the aliens was basically non-existent.

And they had no weapons. They had never been smart enough to create any.

Just their sheer mass and ability to breed was their weapon. And that was enough.

Now, for sixteen years, every resource humanity in hundreds of galaxies could muster quickly was headed here or had gotten here after being retrofitted with the new trans-tunnel drive.

The ship *Star Mist* was on the first front they had outlined at the beginning. Benny and Gina had taken *Star Rain* to a second front and Carrie and Matt had taken *Star Fall* to a third front.

The scientists who had studied the alien transports concluded that the best way to destroy an alien ship was a single, low-intensity weapon into the trans-tunnel drive. The alien ship exploded like a kid's balloon against a cactus.

The idea was to destroy all the ships leaving a galaxy and trap the aliens in one galaxy where they would eventually just turn on each other and die off.

But the aliens had to be contained inside the galaxy and galaxies were damn big things and easy for a tiny ship to escape.

So for sixteen years, Benny didn't want to think about the millions of alien ships they had already destroyed. But as more information flowed and more scouting had been done, it was clear to them all that they were losing the fight.

And they were missing alien ships, letting them through to find new galaxies. With the aliens, all it took was one ship to eventually populate an entire galaxy in just six hundred years.

They bred, as the old saying back in New York was, like rats.

They were rats.

Gina reached over and took Benny's hand as he kept staring at the data pouring across the big screen from the newest scouting missions.

"Let's go find out what Chairmen Ray and Tacita want."

"Almost afraid to," Benny said.

"Yeah, I hear you there," Gina said.

A moment later they had transported two hundred galaxies away to another front of this massive war.

TWO

CARRIE AND MATT from the *Star Fall* were already there and a moment later their hosts, Angie and Gage from *Star Mist* appeared.

The conference room on *Star Mist* looked the same as the one on *Star Fall.* The room was filled in the center by a long oak-colored wooden table that had two large, high-backed black leather chairs on each side and two on each end. The ceiling was high enough for holographic images to form over the table. And the light was all indirect and always just perfect. There were always beverages and snacks along the back wall.

Gina liked the room, but not what they talked about in the room all the time.

Carrie and Matt were also from Benny's home world and had both survived the disaster that killed most of the planet's population. They had both been from the Portland, Oregon, area. Gina liked them both a lot.

Carrie was very short, with long brown hair and skin that looked like it had never seen sun. She had an infectious smile that made people around her laugh.

And yet, at the same time, Carrie was intense and a fighter and Gina decided she would never want to tangle with her.

Matt was about the same height as Gina and Benny and his short brown hair always seemed to be blowing in all directions at once. He seemed to mostly just sit and listen, but when he said something, it tended to cut right to the problem.

Carrie and Matt sat across the wide table from Benny and Gina.

Ray and Tacita looked as they always looked, a black silk shirt for Ray and pantsuit for Tacita. Ray had long, gray hair going down his back and Tacita kept her black hair starkly short.

They were the oldest Seeders by far and had been the first chairman of a mother ship over four million years ago. That was a number that Gina had a hard time even trying to imagine.

She had no idea how two people could live four million years and not be bored or senile. It seemed the special Seeder gene allowed them to remember better and just live forever, barring accidents.

Ray and Tacita sat in their normal seats at the other end of the table opposite Angie and Gage.

Angie had long black hair she kept pulled back and was tall and thin and clearly in shape. She had also come from Benny's home world. Gage was about the same height as Gina and Benny and had a short, military haircut. He had been in the Seeders responsible for helping the planet recover and had rescued Angie one day and they had been in love ever since.

Gina liked them both a lot. Solid, very, very competent people.

"I think we are ready," Angie said.

Gina glanced at Ray and Tacita at the other end of the table as they both nodded. Gina had to admit that Ray and Tacita had moved mountains in this fight so far and never seemed to tire bringing fighter crews from the Milky Way.

And in these meetings, Angie could never tell if they were bringing good news or bad news.

"Thank you for the meeting and sorry for the short notice," Ray said.

"We assumed you would want to know this," Tacita said.

None of them said a word, letting Ray go on.

"First, as discussed in the last chairmen's meeting on the original Earth, we have seven more mother ships coming in this direction, all fitted with the new drives. And more are clearing their current tasks, retrofitting their drives and will be starting in this direction as well over the next one hundred years."

Gina just shook her head slightly. Seeders not only thought in very large distances, galaxy-spanning distances, often treating galaxies like way-stops or measuring marks along the way, but they also planned in centuries of time. The fact that this fight had been going on now for so long was only a tiny blip to longer-lived Seeders.

"All mother ships have also retrofitted their bays to build and hold only the military mother ships. By the time they arrive each will have thousands more ships to add to the front lines and they are building more every day."

Gina was very glad to hear that again. She and Benny and everyone at the table knew that information already, but it sure felt good to hear once again that a lot more ships were coming to help in this seemingly hopeless fight.

"And fighters from younger galaxies?" Gage asked.

"We are recruiting and training from everywhere," Ray said. "The entire branch of Seeders who helped new recruits has grown into the largest area of all Seeders in just ten years. And we are scanning a thousand seeded planets a week for Seeder genes in the populations."

Gina nodded. She didn't want to ask how many they were finding. It seemed that Seeder genes were very rare things. But there was no doubt the war effort was clearly gearing up on a scale almost impossible to imagine. That was good news, but not news that would be at the level of an emergency meeting.

"A second update before we give you the reason we asked for this meeting," Ray said. "The last of the transit jump stations will be coming online in two weeks."

"Wonderful," Benny said.

Everyone nodded.

Gina agreed. That was good news because the jump stations were a series of stations spaced just the right distance apart so that any Seeder could jump to this area of the known universe, going from one station to the next. She and Benny could jump vast distances because of their training and special gene. But most Seeders had a range of just about 100,000 light years, about the breadth of the Milky Way Galaxy back home.

So to build a jump station from the Seeder-settled part of the universe to here, there were thousands and thousands of jump stations along the track. Building that had been a massive undertaking and Gina, in the beginning, never thought it would be built in time to help.

She had been wrong, clearly.

And she was damn glad she had been.

That meant far more ships could be built here, near the lines and crews could come to their ships without Ray and Tacita having to jump them.

"The big news we have is that we finally have working the extreme long-range scanner," Tacita said.

Gina about came out of her chair. Sixteen years they had been waiting for a scanner that would spot any alien ship even a hundred thousand light years away.

"The scanner will show all alien and human ships in motion within a two-hundred-thousand light-year radius."

"With your permissions," Ray said, "we would like to give the details on building the scanner to your ships."

"It is designed to also work with boosters to expand the range," Tacita said, "so before the system is turned on completely, we will need for ships to spread boosters around to certain locations along all front lines."

"And to the second and third lines of defense as well," Benny said.

"Exactly," Ray said, nodding.

Gina was excited and she could see that Benny was as well. Now, maybe, just maybe, they could see who they were fighting instead of having to just stumble into them in the dark of space.

"And we hope to set up a wall of monitoring stations between this area of space and human-settled areas," Ray said. "That will take a few hundred years to accomplish, but worth the price and safety. The work has already started."

Gina nodded to that as well, as did everyone else.

"How long until the scanners are fully operational in this area?" Gage asked a moment before Gina could ask the exact same question.

"Two years considering all lines of defenses and the time it will take to build and plant the boosters," Ray said.

"But we can test it on galaxies near your ships as soon as your ships have integrated it into their scanning systems," Tacita said.

Ray nodded. "We suggest we do that first before moving forward."

Gina glanced around at the other five chairmen. All of them were nodding.

She smiled at Benny. This could mean the turning point in this fight since over the last sixteen years, the hardest part was just finding the alien ships between galaxies. They missed so many. It had felt at times as if they were taking cups of water out of a waterfall in hopes of stopping the torrent.

Benny nodded and smiled as well, then turned to Ray and Tacita. "Please work with *Star Fall* to get the new scanning system in place."

"And with *Star Mist*," Angie said and Gage nodded.

"And with *Star Rain*," Carrie said.

For the first time in a lot of years, Gina felt hopeful that they might have a chance to win this fight.

Or at least slow the expansion down enough to get the full weight of galaxies full of humanity working on the problem in time.

THREE

BENNY HAD BEEN excited since Ray and Tacita brought the long-range scanner with them. It seemed that the two inventors of the new trans-tunnel drive had been challenged by the idea of trying to scan for a tiny dot and energy signature from hundreds of thousands of light years away.

The two inventors had been spending the entire time, sixteen years, on the task. As had thousands of other scientists, but it had been those two who had made the breakthrough by using brand new scanning technology that worked in the trans-tunnel space looking for disruptions.

"The scanning system on all three ships are tested and working," *Star Rain* told them four weeks after the meeting with Ray and Tacita.

Star Rain always spoke to Benny and Gina in a solid, female voice and everyone thought of *Star Rain* as female, even though Benny doubted an intelligent computer thought in terms of gender.

Now it was time to test the new scanner. Benny felt even more excited. Finally, they were going to be able to see what they were fighting.

Finally, after sixteen years.

Benny wasn't sure he wanted to see. But he had to.

They all did.

He and Gina were in their command chair and linked with the other chairmen on the other two mother ships. As always, in the command chair, they held hands and the heads-up displays flowed past them.

While in the chair, Benny felt at times as if he and Gina were in each other's minds. He loved that.

And he could sense *Star Rain* as well.

"*Star Rain,*" Gina asked, "how will we be able to tell the difference between an alien ship and a human ship?"

"Alien ships will be designated by a red dot, Seeder ships designated by a green dot, other human ships from The Creators and The Exterminators designated by blue."

"We are ready," Gina said.

"So are we," Carrie said.

Benny could hear the excitement in their voices matching his own.

"How about we scan part of our area first," Gage said. "Since we have been trying to stop them here the longest."

All agreed, since the mother ships were too far apart to even come close to overlapping scans at this point. Benny knew that being able to do that would still be a year or more away and would take a lot of signal boosters being built.

"Do we have any boosters online yet?" Angie asked *Star Mist.*

"There are enough boosters online to cover the thirty closest active alien galaxies to this position along what is being called the front line," *Star Mist* replied to all the chairmen.

Benny liked the sound of that.

"Good," Gage said. "All right, let's take a look. And *Star Mist,* keep the image only for chairmen at the moment."

"First only show Seeder ships and designate this ship with a slightly brighter point," Angie said.

Damn, Benny found this so exciting he had to force himself to breathe.

Gina squeezed his hand and took a deep breath as well.

A hologram of the area of space along the front line appeared in front of Benny and Gina.

Benny was surprised at how many thousands of small green dots appeared around *Star Mist*'s position in space.

It seemed as if their coverage was very tight, but he knew those ships were hundreds of light years from the closest ship, some far more. And without this scanner, up until now they only had short-range scanners of less than a quarter of a light year to try to find an alien ship.

On the left were the alien occupied galaxies, on the right were the galaxies they were trying to protect from the alien ships.

"*Star Mist,* now add in the alien ships," Angie said.

The entire hologram almost turned completely red.

Angie gasped.

Gina clamped down on Benny's hand.

Benny said simply, "Shit."

It was a massive sea of millions and millions of alien ships. And a lot of the red dots were into the galaxies behind the front line.

Benny felt sick.

"We are so screwed," Gage said.

Benny could only agree with that.

"Let's see what it looks like around *Star Rain*," Angie said, her voice almost hollow.

The horrid image vanished and once again Benny forced himself to take a deep breath.

A second hologram appeared in front of them, showing the Seeder ships and *Star Rain.* Again it seemed like a decent defense line.

"*Star Rain,* please add in the alien ships," Benny said.

Again the entire hologram seemed to turn a bright shade of red. And the galaxies beyond the front lines were filled with red dots as well.

Benny just wanted to hit something, but instead he just sat there.

The same thing repeated around *Star Fall.*

And these images showed only a tiny, tiny part of the battle area. They wouldn't have the full picture for years yet until all the scanner boosters were put into place.

But it was clear from where Benny sat.

They were losing this war.

As far as he knew, they had already lost it.

FOUR

GINA STOOD beside their chairmen's chair in the command center, just sort of staring at the big screen and thinking. Benny was off having a quick meeting with some military mother-ship chairmen and he was going to meet her back here at any moment.

On the screen in front of her it showed the area of space they had been trying to defend, mostly covered with red alien ships.

For the three years after the first scans, humanity had geared up even more. It seemed that Ray and Tacita were moving mountains, if not entire galaxies, to join the fight. They were pushing to get every bit of fighting power to these front lines.

Gina was impressed and it seemed that those first scans had scared them more than anyone.

Anyone with a brain knew how scary an infestation like this was. Like a bad infection in a human body could spread, this infection, if not contained at this level, could spread over all the known universe. And at full force, even a galaxy of humans could not stop the wave of rats pouring at them.

After three years, new military ship factories were coming online almost every week around this sector of space.

And all effort was put to building booster scanners and linking in all fighting ships to the scans so they would know if there was an alien ship close to them.

The kill rate of alien ships had jumped dramatically with the ability to see them. The small military ten-man fighters were now being called Sharks because they could take out an alien ship and jump and ten minutes later take out another.

But Gina and everyone on every ship knew they were still losing.

One alien planet alone in a galaxy could pour out millions and millions of transport ships over a fifty-year period, continuing until every bit of material on the planet was exhausted.

You multiply that by maybe a billion planets in just a normal-sized galaxy and

hundreds of years and the number became a staggering wave of red.

Gina still felt mostly discouraged at the progress. But after three years they finally had all the area inside the million galaxies in this area monitored in one way or another.

So they at least knew how bad they were losing.

Benny's secondary line of defense which was to protect the galaxies beyond the main line of defense seemed to be on full push as well. But it took far more firepower to destroy a growing infestation on a planet then it did a transport ship in space. So the decision had been made to follow Seeder guidelines and just let the civilization grow once it was started on a planet. But a number of Sharks would be stationed in orbit to make sure no alien ship left the planet's gravity well.

But in every galaxy there could be a billion alien planets. Once infected to any extent, that line of defense flat didn't work.

But on new infections into a galaxy, that plan of Sharks in orbit tended to stop the growth inside of new galaxies when caught early. But they often didn't see a new planet starting to launch ships until the ships were in space and able to be picked up on the scanners.

And often the ship wasn't in space very long jumping between planets, so even with the scanning technology, they didn't have the firepower or even awareness to track everything.

Gina knew, as all of them did, that they were still decades, if not a hundred years or more from having enough ships to even begin to battle this growing infestation on a level basis.

They were slowing the spread, but only slowing it.

And not by that much.

Very discouraging.

The third line of defense was also catching ships now that they could see them.

At one point a few months back, they had decided to set up yet a fourth line of defense much farther out, just to be sure. The sensors for that were being built now.

And Ray and Tacita reported that the sensor shield and thousands of ships were now manning the protection line between this area of space and human occupied space. Even though it would take an alien ship thousands of years to make that journey with the old trans-tunnel drives they used, no one wanted to take a chance that just one ship would get through.

Angie felt good about that at least.

Over the last year, two more Seeder mother ships had arrived as well. But the chairmen of both had no battle experience, so even though considerably older, they chose to let the six chairmen of the three main ships be in charge of the entire operation.

So the weight of all this rested on the six of them. And Gina felt it every day. And she knew Benny did as well.

This was going to be a very, very long fight.

SECTION TWO
The Empty Space Problem

FIVE

BENNY AND GINA were in their command chair, studying the battle scenes as more sensors came online. Behind them, the huge command center ran with muffled talking and an efficiency Benny always found impressive. They had the best and most dedicated command crew anyone could ever hope for.

And all of them were focused completely on the task at hand, even though they all knew they would be at this for maybe a century or more.

Star Rain fed Benny and Gina information both through non-verbal connections and heads-up displays. The situation had just gotten worse and worse as each day went by, especially now that they actually knew where more and more of the alien ships were.

And it seemed like every day more sensors came onto the network showing millions more alien ships.

Benny hated the impossible feeling of what they were facing. As Carrie had said a number of years back, they couldn't miss a single alien ship. But from the sensors they now had online, the rough count of alien ships was far over eighty billion.

He couldn't even imagine that number.

And every day that count seemed to climb instead of go down, even with thousands and thousands of Seeder ships destroying alien ships. It seemed more alien ships were launched from hundreds of millions of planets than Seeder ships could destroy by factors.

The initial mission of the three mother ships to this distant area of space had been to find out about an alien culture. A solo alien ship had reached the edge of human occupied space with its alien occupants long dead. The ship had been traveling for over two hundred thousand years. So no one knew what to expect at the origin of that alien ship.

With the new trans-tunnel drive and exploring along the way, it had taken thirteen years for the three mother ships, *Star Rain, Star Mist,* and *Star Fall* to reach the alien area of space.

When they had first gotten to this area of space, they had discovered hundreds and hundreds of completely destroyed galaxies. It seemed the branch of humanity that had created this mess was trying to destroy the aliens by firebombing every alien planet in an entire galaxy.

But usually by the time The Creators, as they called themselves, had gotten to a galaxy to destroy it, the aliens had already sent out hundreds of millions of ships from that galaxy to infect millions more galaxies.

So when the three mother ships had arrived and learned what was happening, the decision had been made to not even contact The Creators. Or the group that had followed them millions of years before called "The Exterminators." Since both ancient groups still had old, slow drives, it was decided they would be more trouble than they would be help.

The decision of the Seeders was to let the aliens left behind on planets just die off naturally. It seemed the aliens took every resource a planet had to build ships and those left behind on the planet were without food and resources and turned on each other and quickly died off.

So the Seeders had taken the fight to the vastness of space between the galaxies to stop the aliens in space. That had been Benny's idea. But now he was starting to think that idea had no hope.

"*Rescue One* has arrived in the area of *Star Mist,*" *Star Rain* reported to them.

Benny glanced at the specs on the newly arrived ship as they scrolled over his display.

Rescue One was half the size of a mother ship and the chairman was named Evan West. *Rescue One* had been upgrad-ed to the new trans-tunnel drive and in the ten-year trip here from human space, it had built complete hangars full of the large military ships and a couple thousand smaller Sharks.

And they had brought the crew for all of the ships as well as the crew for another two hundred ships yet to be built here.

"Wow," Gina said. "That's going to help some."

Benny wanted to say that it wouldn't make a dent, but he didn't. Gina and the other four chairmen who were running this knew exactly how bad the situation was. They were kids on a beach with sand pails trying to stop a tsunami. He didn't need to make things worse by running off his mouth.

Then a bit of data about the new arrival went over his screen. It seemed the *Rescue One* got its name when it was built to save the mother ship *Dreaming Large* from empty space.

He didn't remember learning anything about that.

Now all Seeder ships just had automatic sensors and avoided the small, solar-system-sized bubbles of null or empty space. He did a quick scan of the story about *Dreaming Large.*

It was thanks to that rescue operation the sensors for null space had been invented for every Seeder ship. Before then, Seeder ships just vanished, often not appearing again for hundreds of thousands of years, even though on the ship only a few hours had passed.

Suddenly Benny realized something else they were missing.

Something major.

Empty space.

Damn, just damn.

He brought back up the image of the fifty or so galaxies closest to their position on his and Gina's display. As always, there were a few thousand Seeder ships showing green in a sea of alien red ships. Even though the area shown was more than a hundred million light years across, it still looked like it was covered in solid red.

Gina glanced at him. He could sense she was puzzled at what he was doing.

"*Rescue One* reminded me we are missing something very, very critical in this fight," he said. "*Star Rain,* please show in bright white dots all the empty space areas in this scan."

The white dots spread out solidly through the entire area of space.

"Oh, no," Gina said, clearly catching on to what he was thinking.

"*Star Rain,*" Benny said, "Approximately, to the nearest thousand, how many empty space areas are showing?"

"Over eighty-six thousand," *Star Rain* said.

"*Star Rain,*" Gina said, "Would you have any way to estimate how many alien ships have been lost in an empty space bubble?"

"In this area shown?" *Star Rain* asked.

"Yes," Benny said. "In the area shown."

"Approximately nine thousand," *Star Rain* said.

"Could you extrapolate that over the entire history of the alien race expansion," Gina asked. "Very rough and approximate would be fine."

"Aliens have been expanding for 280 thousand years," *Star Rain* said. "In that amount of time, an estimation of alien ships vanishing into null space would be approximately two hundred million."

"Two hundred million?" Gina asked.

"Approximately," *Star Rain* said.

"We are so screwed," Benny said, his stomach in a knot as he stared at the screen of red with white dots. And he had thought the battle had been impossible ten minutes ago.

"We can't miss a ship," Gina said softly.

"Even one that might just reappear two hundred thousand years from now," Benny said.

Gina laughed, but it sounded forced. "At least they are out of our way for now."

Benny laughed. But she did have a point.

SIX

GINA HATED more than she wanted to think about the empty space problem Benny had just noticed. She had been managing to hold out hope that given enough time and forces, they could slow and then eventually stop the alien expansion.

She knew that was only a hope, and not based on any kind of probability. After the first group of sensors came online, Benny had asked *Star Rain* to calculate the odds of defeating the alien expansion.

Star Rain's answer had been zero percent. Not even a tiny fraction chance of success. Benny had decided he would never ask that question again, but he still did every six months or so.

He just put his head down and worked on the problem, something she loved about him. One of the many hundreds of things she loved about him, actually. No task seemed impossible to him if he worked at it hard enough.

Now this had just made things worse. Much worse.

One alien ship finding a galaxy and this infection would start all over. Just one.

"We need to tell the others," Benny said after the two of them had gone back over the data even more about how many alien ships were trapped in empty space, just waiting like time-bombs to come out and infect things all over again.

"Not going to be a fun meeting," she said.

"How about we get Chairman West in on the meeting to help us understand everything," Benny said, standing.

Gina stood as well and stretched. "But let's talk with the other four first, so they are not caught by surprise with this."

Benny nodded, then said, "*Star Rain,* would you contact the Chairmen of *Star Fall* and *Star Mist* and ask for an emergency meeting on *Star Mist?*"

"Be glad to," *Star Rain* said.

A moment later *Star Rain* said, "They have agreed. On *Star Mist.*"

"Thank you," Gina said.

A moment later she and Benny were standing in the *Star Mist* conference room more millions of light-years away from *Star Fall* than she wanted to think about.

The large oak-colored wooden table filled the center of the conference room and Gina and Benny took their normal seats along one side in the comfortable dark-leather chairs. She could smell some cookies and cupcakes already on the table at the back, but at the moment she didn't feel up for a snack. Not with this news they were about to hand to the others.

Carrie and Matt appeared a moment later and sat across from Gina and Benny. Both Carrie and Matt were dressed comfortably in jeans and light shirts.

Gina loved the lack of any dress code about the Seeders. There was never a thought about dressing other than for comfort. She and Benny were seldom in anything but jeans, dress shirts, and tennis shoes. Sure made dressing every morning easier.

"Even more problems, huh?" Matt asked, smiling as he sat down.

"They never seem to end," Benny said, smiling as well.

"Oh, super," Carrie said, laughing. "And just when some major reinforcements arrived."

"Yeah," Benny said, "that illustrated the problem."

Gina loved the attitude of the six of them. They all knew it was impossible, what they were trying to do, but they didn't let that get to their attitudes.

At that moment Angie and Gage appeared and sat at the head of the large table.

"More fun, huh?" Gage asked.

"A real party," Benny said.

"So we noticed that the *Rescue One* had arrived," Gina said, deciding to get right to the point.

"Bringing a bunch of military ships and Sharks," Gage said, nodding. "We all just need to figure out how to deploy all of them."

Everyone nodded, but waited for Gina to go on.

"*Rescue One* is known for saving the mother ship *Dreaming Large* from an empty space bubble," Gina said.

"And giving all Seeder ships a scanning system to spot empty space bubbles and avoid them," Benny said.

"Oh, shit," Gage said, sitting back.

Gina nodded. Clearly Gage had jumped to exactly what they had figured out.

"May I have *Star Mist* put up a hologram of this area of space?" Gina asked.

Angie nodded, looking puzzled at Gage who just sat there staring at the ceiling.

"Star Mist, would you please show a hologram of the closest 50 galaxies along this line of defense?"

"I would be glad to," *Star Mist* said and the hologram appeared. It looked so clean with just the dots of lights.

"Please show all alien ships in this area of space," Gina said. She didn't really want to see this again for this area, but they all had to.

The clean image became filled with more millions of red dots than Gina wanted to think about it.

"Please, *Star Mist,"* Gina said, "would you show the locations in bright white dots of the empty space pockets in this area?"

The white lights appeared, dotted all over the area and all through the red dots of alien ships.

"Oh, no," Angie said.

Carrie and Matt were just sitting back, staring at the hologram, their mouths open and their eyes wide.

"Star Mist," Gina said, "could you estimate, roughly, the number of alien ships in this scanned area likely to now be caught in empty space pockets?"

"Over ten thousand," *Star Mist* said. "Rough estimation and rounded."

"Thank you, *Star Mist,"* Gina said.

Everyone was silent just staring at the hologram full of red and the bright white lights showing pockets of empty space.

"Star Rain estimates," Gina said, "that we could have over two hundred million alien ships trapped in empty space pockets since the beginning of the alien expansion."

"Do you agree with that number, *Star Mist?"* Angie asked.

"Yes," *Star Mist* said. "Many factors are in the equation, but taking into account the time of alien expansion and location of many of the empty space bubbles, that number might be slightly low."

Silence filled the conference room as all six of them sat staring at the sector of space filled with red dots of alien ships.

Finally Angie said, "Thank you, *Star Mist.* You can shut down the image."

The image of hopelessness hanging over the table vanished and Gina found herself taking a deep breath.

"I'm so glad you wanted to share this news," Gage said, shaking his head.

"That's what friends are for," Benny said, smiling.

They all laughed. Not one thing else they could do.

SEVEN

BENNY LIKED Chairman Evan West of *Rescue One* right from the start. West was a tall, thin man with bright green eyes and a balding head. From his record, he was thousands of years old, which had Benny intimidated almost from the start.

But when Chairman West transported to the meeting room to talk with the six of them, he was charming and kept the mood light to start. He took a chair at the end of the table facing Angie and Gage.

And West was very, very respectful to all of them, even though combined they hadn't lived a third of his age. That didn't seem to bother him in the slightest.

When he first arrived, it was clear to Benny that Chairman West thought he was here to talk about how to deploy his ships and forces. And they would have that meeting in time.

So when Angie asked him to explain to them the nature of empty space, he looked surprised.

"Your arrival has made us realize we have a problem," Gage said.

"A larger problem than the impossible one we already face," Benny said.

"Yeah, that too," Gage said.

West chuckled, but Benny could tell he was suddenly worried.

"We think," Gage said, "that we have over two hundred million alien ships in empty space bubbles."

West started to say something, then stopped, his mouth open.

Benny could see that suddenly the obvious that they had all missed hit West solidly. No one, since his rescue of *Dreaming Large,* thought much at all about empty space. Like a moon or an asteroid belt, it was just something to not hit.

"We can't let one ship escape," Angie said.

"One ship can contaminate an entire galaxy in just over six hundred years," Carrie said, "and launch more hundreds and hundreds of millions of alien ships into space than we want to think about."

"So we need a lesson on empty space bubbles to know what we are facing," Benny said.

Benny watched as Chairman West just blinked for a moment.

"How they are formed, do they serve a purpose, how can we destroy one, and so on," Angie said.

West nodded and took a deep breath.

Benny was impressed. This guy had lived a very long time, but it was clear to Benny he had never been under this kind of stress before, except maybe in the rescue of *Dreaming Large.*

"I can download to your ships from *Rescue One* all data we gathered and details," West said, "to the tiniest detail on how we freed *Dreaming Large.*"

"Would you do that now," Angie asked. "We need to have our ships with all this information as soon as possible."

West nodded and contacted his second in command and had that done.

A few moments later *Star Mist* said, "Receiving the information now."

Benny contacted *Star Rain* and Carrie contacted *Star Fall* to make sure the information was coming in there as well.

"So," Gina said after a moment, facing Chairman West, "what exactly is empty space?"

"It is, basically," West said, taking a deep breath and focusing on the topic at hand, "exactly what its name implies. It is an area devoid of all space and time. Normal space around us has many things in it, but inside the gravitational bubble of empty space, nothing exists, including most laws of physics."

Benny tried to image that and failed, so decided to ask the next question.

"How does a bubble like that even exist? What creates it?"

"Universal forces of gravity create them," West said. "Every object in the universe warps time and space around it. When certain sets of gravitational forces come into play with each other, the forces form neutral areas and these neutral areas form as gravitational bubbles of nothingness."

Benny shook his head, still not following completely.

"So back on our home world," Matt said, "we had high-speed roads for traffic. These roads formed all sorts of patterns to allow vehicles to get on and off smoothly. But there were always dead, worthless areas inside those interchanges, those patterns."

West nodded. "My home world had those as well. Those dead areas would be these empty space areas. Gravitational forces are in play around a dead area like traffic on an exchange and form the bubble around the nothingness. Once formed it takes on a stability all its own."

Benny shook his head and smiled at Matt. "Thank you. Just saved me a giant headache trying to understand these things."

"I was going there myself," Matt said, smiling.

"Think of them like a balloon," West said. "To save the *Dreaming Large,* we had to let in regular space and time evenly from all directions at the same time."

"So if we just blow a hole in the side of one of these empty spaces?" Benny asked.

"Real time and space and gravitational forces would rush in and destroy anything inside the bubble," West said.

"So we need to pop a lot of bubbles," Benny said, nodding. Maybe, just maybe not all was lost yet.

"We can do that," Gage said and the other chairmen nodded.

"For every bubble you pop," West said, shaking his head, "another might appear to balance things. It seems the bubbles are also used to balance gravitational forces in an area. Or at least that's the theory. Never been tested. Until now there was no reason to test it."

"When you destroyed the bubble around *Dreaming Large,* did another one form?" Angie asked.

West nodded. "About thirty light-years away and almost swallowed another Seeder ship before we realized what was happening and got the ship out of the way."

Benny just shook his head. Nothing at all was easy about any of this.

EIGHT

GINA AND BENNY had alternated cooking from the moment they had met. They both liked to cook and it gave them time away. They both tried to protect their private time and get full nights sleep every night. And dinner was part of that.

This evening it was Gina's turn and she was working on a pasta salad and chicken breasts smothered in Italian spices. One of the advantages they had being on a ship the size of a moon, there was lots of room to grow fresh vegetables and chicken and fish.

The kitchen in their chairmen's quarters was a dream kitchen as far as she was concerned, with stone-like counter tops, two large sinks, and enough area to prepare anything she or Benny felt like preparing.

Off to one side of the kitchen was a wonderful dining room that could sit eight at the beautiful wooden maple dining table, but they kept the table downsized so she and Benny could sit facing each other and talk across a small table.

They had decorated their apartment with pictures of her home planet and New York City on his home world, where they had lived together for the first two years and tried to help survivors of what they called The Event.

It had been a hard two years, scrambling for food and trying to keep the spirits of those around them up. Even though at any point they could have gone to one of the Seeder ships in orbit, they chose to stay on the surface.

So now those images of her home world and his decorated their wonderful apartment. And in the nearby living room they often cuddled on the couch and watched old movies. She had a lot of movies from his world to catch up on and he had a lot of movies from hers. It was great fun.

She was almost finished with preparing dinner and was about to call Benny when he came out of his office and leaned against the counter to watch her.

"Anything I can do to help?" he asked. "It smells wonderful."

"Just sit down," she said, laughing.

They went through that exact same routine every night, the one not cooking asking at the last minute if they could help. She loved that ritual.

"So what were you working on?" she asked as she first dished up the pasta salad.

"Trying to see if I can understand these empty space bubbles a little more," he said.

"And do you?" she asked, as she put the chicken on a plate for each of them and decorated it with steamed spears of asparagus.

"I think I do," he said as she served them both and sat down. "But can't seem to find an answer to one really stupid question."

He shook his head and dug into the salad.

"What question," she asked.

"Can we move the things," he said.

She sort of froze, the first bite of chicken halfway to her mouth.

"Move them?"

"Great chicken," he said, nodding.

"Thank you," she said, finishing getting the bite to her mouth. And he was right, it had come out wonderfully, with an Italian spice that gave it just a little zest but kept the chicken flavor.

"So why move them?" she asked.

"Something you said earlier," Benny said. "If we could get more alien ships to run into the empty space on their own, we could slow them down and then we come along later and pop the bubble and destroy bunches of them all at the same time."

She just stared at the man she loved more than anything. He looked more military than anything, yet his mind worked in ways that constantly astounded her.

He could see things that made no sense to anyone else.

"Also trying to see if we could make them bigger," he said. "Bigger rat traps."

She just kept staring at him. Both of those ideas just might work. Both were brilliant and might turn the tide if they did work.

He shrugged and kept eating. "Silly damn idea considering the size of space between galaxies."

She just kept staring at him until he noticed and stopped eating and said, "What? I got food stuck to my nose or something?"

She laughed. "No, just admiring that brain of yours is all."

He laughed. "I'll let you admire other parts of this body later if you want."

"Once I get past admiring the brain," she said, smiling at him, "I just might."

NINE

BENNY AND GINA the next morning in their command chair, after going over all the reports coming in from scouts and Sharks destroying alien ships, decided to dig more into the idea of moving one of the empty space bubbles.

They had talked about it more last night and both spent time in their offices after dinner making sure they understood what these empty space bubbles actually were.

As far as Benny could tell, they were exactly as Chairman West described them. Nothingness. Complete. No time, no gravity, nothing, held together by a gravity bubble membrane of some sort.

And the more they researched it, the more excited Benny got that this might not be another problem, but in fact might be another weapon for them in the fight to stop the alien expansion.

So now after a good night's sleep, they sat in their command chair ready to try to figure it all out.

"Star Rain?" Benny asked, "would it be possible to move an empty space bubble?"

"In theory, yes," *Star Rain* said.

Since they were in their command chair, he was holding Gina's hand and he squeezed it in excitement of that answer.

She squeezed back.

"Would it be possible to expand the size of an existing empty space bubble?" Gina asked.

"In theory, yes," *Star Rain* said.

Benny almost felt like jumping up out of the chair and doing a little dance. But he had one more question.

"Star Rain, would it be possible to create from scratch an empty space bubble?"

"In theory, yes," *Star Rain* said.

Benny had to get up and so did Gina. They both stood and paced in front of their chair, making many of the command crew look down at them with puzzled looks. But since both were smiling, the command crew, rightfully, decided to not say anything. At that moment, Benny appreciated that.

"Before we go one more step down the road on this," Gina said, finally stopping in front of Benny, smiling, "we need to see if the size of space the alien ships are traveling through would even make such a thing worthwhile to us."

"Agreed," Benny said. *"Star Rain,* on the big screen, please illustrate an alien occupied galaxy with most of the alien inhabited planets in the galaxy producing alien ships. Any of the galaxies that fit that parameter would be fine."

In front of them on the wall-sized screen a three dimensional image of a spiral galaxy appeared. It looked a lot like the Milky Way, only about two-thirds the size from the statistics being shown on the screen.

"How many alien planets in this galaxy?" Gina asked.

The Creators had designed this rat-like race to need a similar planet than humans needed under a yellow star in what was the habitable temperature zone orbit. So that limited the number of planets a great deal.

"Approximately six-point-one billion," *Star Rain* said.

"How many alien ships are leaving this galaxy in a twenty-four-hour period?" Gina asked.

"One-point-four million," *Star Rain* said.

Benny just shook his head. Maybe it would be better to just go in and destroy every planet in the galaxy as The Creators and The Exterminators were trying to do. But he couldn't stomach that and he knew most Seeders could not either, unless it was a last resort.

But at these numbers, unless they found some way to slow down those ships and the alien expansion, Seeders may not have a choice.

"Would you please show, if possible, the general path of most of the ships?" Gina asked.

"Alien ships are designed, from what we have learned from the Creator's files," *Star Rain* said, "to first find the closest planet to settle and then the closest galaxy. In a simple view, these are the three main paths the majority of alien ships are taking from this galaxy."

The image on the screen shifted to looking down on the galaxy as if it were just in two dimensions. The red dots of alien ships formed three wide streams, going in three directions from the galaxy toward three other galaxies.

Benny just damn near fell over.

"Holy shit," a voice echoed through the room from the command crew behind them.

Benny couldn't agree more.

"So we can predict them to a degree," Gina said, nodding to Benny and smiling.

He just stood there staring at the screen. Then he asked the question he didn't want to ask.

"How wide and how deep are each of those streams of alien ships, approximately?"

Benny was holding his breath waiting for the answer and he bet everyone in the command center behind him was doing the same.

"Each stream is approximately the same width as the galaxy, or 100,000 light years wide," *Star Rain* said, "and the same depth as the galaxy of about 8,000 light years."

"How long is the travel time for an alien ship?" Gina asked. "Please indicate in approximate years near each stream on the screen."

On the screen Benny could see the answer. One stream took approximately 27 years for each ship to get to the next galaxy. Another stream took 30 years, and a third stream took 34 years.

"*Star Rain*," Benny said, "In theory, could we make an empty space bubble a full light year across?"

"In theory, yes," *Star Rain* said.

"How big could we go?" Gina asked.

"There is a stabilization point," *Star Rain* said. "Any size would be possible, in theory, if that stabilization point in the area of the empty space bubble was maintained."

"Holy shit," Benny said to himself.

Gina just grabbed him and kissed him.

Then she turned and said to everyone in the command center, "Go back to work. We'll brief you all on this as soon as we know more."

"*Star Rain*," Benny said, "Could you ask the other four chairmen for an emergency meeting again. And ask them to invite Chairman West."

A moment later *Star Rain* said, "They have agreed."

"Here we go," Gina said.

"I just hope we don't waste too many resources on this," Benny said, suddenly feeling worried. This idea was totally crazy and right now they couldn't afford to go wasting resources in a wrong direction.

"Can we stop a million-plus ships a day just from this one galaxy?" Gina asked.

Benny shook his head. They couldn't even stop a fraction of them, even knowing where they were. And that was only one small galaxy.

"So no idea is too wild to explore," she said, smiling at him. "Even one of yours."

"Thanks," he said, laughing and shaking his head. "I think."

He just hoped to hell she was right.

Now Available
from all your favorite booksellers in trade paper and electronic editions.

DEAN WESLEY
SMITH

USA Today BESTSELLING AUTHOR

MONUMENTAL
SUMMIT

A SCIENCE FICTION NOVEL OF THE OLD WEST AND TRUE LOVE

SECTION THREE
The Shape of Empty Space

TEN

GINA AND BENNY had presented what they had discovered and thought about to the other chairmen in the meeting room on *Star Mist*.

At first, the other chairmen had just sat there, stunned. Chairman West just sort of nodded the more they got into their presentation.

Gina and Benny could hardly contain their excitement and Gina could tell the excitement seemed to slowly be catching with the others. These empty-space pockets might not be a huge problem, but instead a weapon.

Then Gage asked simply, once Benny and Gina were finished, "Is this possible?"

"*Star Rain* says it is in theory," Gina said.

All six looked at West.

He shrugged. "Empty space pockets tend to be a certain size, but not all of them. I have seen empty space pockets smaller than a moon and others twenty times the size of the one that caught *Dreaming Large.*"

"*Star Mist,*" Angie said, "Would you consult with *Star Rain* and *Star Fall* to determine the parameters possible for an empty space bubble?"

"We agree that any size is theoretically possible," *Star Mist* said. "But past a certain size the bubble would only exist for a fraction of a second."

"What is that theoretical size of stability?" Gage asked.

"A diameter of just over one hundred light years," *Star Mist* said.

Gina felt shocked. Putting an empty space bubble that size in the middle of those three major streams would catch millions and millions of alien ships each and actually give the Sharks a chance at slowing down and destroying the remaining ships.

"*Star Mist,* could we create one that size?" Matt asked.

"In theory," *Star Mist* said.

"Do you three ships have any idea or theories on how that could be accomplished?" Angie asked.

"No," *Star Mist* said.

Gina did not like the sound of the finality of that statement. But it didn't seem to bother West in the slightest.

"Let me get my original *Dreaming Large* rescue team on this," he said. "They are the best experts there are on empty space. I'll pull them all back together from all over the human universe. We'll find the answer."

"And moving the smaller ones would help as well," Benny said.

West nodded.

Gina understood what Benny was thinking. He had thought about just sending numbers of the small empty space pockets moving back along a stream from a galaxy, catching ships as it went. He had called it "bowling for aliens" and she had kissed him for that silliness.

But underneath the silliness, it was a good idea.

"Once I distribute the fighting forces I brought with me," West said, jumping into action, "with your permissions,

I would like to set up my ship to be the ground center on this research."

Gina glanced around and all were nodding.

"Please do so," Angie said after checking with all the chairmen.

"I will get in touch with Chairmen Ray and Tacita and get their help as well," West said.

Gina could hear the growing excitement in his voice.

Clearly Benny could as well. "You think this is possible?" Benny asked.

West shrugged. "If *Star Mist* and your other ships say it is theoretically possible, then all we have to do is find out how to change that theoretical to reality. It took us a lot of years to go from knowing nothing about empty space to saving a mother ship from it. I think we can do this as well, but it may take years."

"We are going to be at this for years," Gage said, nodding.

Gina agreed with that.

"The more ideas we have to help," Angie said, "the better off we will be in this fight. So thank you, Chairman West, for running with this. Please give us regular updates on your progress."

"Thank you for trusting me with something this important," he said.

They all stood and for the first time in a lot of years, Gina felt lifted by one of the meetings. Everything was still in theory, but theoretical help was more than they had yesterday.

A lot more.

ELEVEN

BENNY STOOD BESIDE their command chair, watching the daily reports of the battle scroll across the big screen. Gina was still in the gym working out as she did three mornings a week, letting him be the first in the Command Center. She liked the extra workout time, said it kept her mind sharp.

Around him the others worked, mostly silently, sometimes conferring with each other in normal voices that seemed almost like whispers down near the command chair the room was so big.

It had been over two years since the meeting about the theory of building large empty space bubbles to trap large numbers of alien ships and Benny had given up counting how many years they had been here blowing alien ships out of space.

Chairman West reported his teams' findings every week on advances in empty space work, but it seemed to Benny to always be the same.

Nothing yet.

Chairmen Ray and Tacita had entire fleets of ships headed this direction, and factories around this area were producing Shark-sized fighting ships at the pace of fifty per day.

The war effort in the last two years had exploded into full movement.

Around Benny, the main command crew was all at stations and working. The entire sphere around the main one hundred and fifty thousand alien-infested galaxies was now under scan, so at least they knew where every alien ship was.

And every alien ship that managed to get outside of that sphere had been destroyed.

But there were far, far too many alien ships to even pretend to deal with, but at least humanity knew where they all were, for what little good that did. Humanity was still losing the battle against the alien expansion and there was talk that in a couple of years they would be forced to fall back to a larger sphere of defense.

That was going to feel like defeat to Benny, but it more than likely was going to have to be done.

Benny was about to turn to talk with their second in command when *Star Rain* said simply, "There is a problem with The Creators' fleet."

Benny glanced back at the big screen. The Creators' ships were working in their area of defense and were always shown as a tiny blob of blue dots moving slowly from galaxy to galaxy. When they reached an alien galaxy, The Creators would fire-bomb every alien planet in the galaxy over a six-week period and then move on, leaving the galaxy a dead husk.

That cleared out and stopped the aliens, but by the time The Creators did that, millions and millions of alien ships had already launched to other galaxies.

Benny considered what The Creators were doing horrid and a total waste of effort. But that was no surprise because The Creators were the same idiots who had started this entire mess with their ideas that they could build an intelligent alien race.

No Seeder had even talked to The Creators. Benny and Gina mostly just ignored them and Benny doubted the Creators even knew the Seeders were here fighting their fight.

The Creators still had the old trans-tunnel drive, so their ships were no faster than the ones they had programmed the aliens to build.

It took Benny a moment of staring at the big screen filling one wall of the command center before he finally understood the problem with The Creators' small fleet of seven-hundred-plus ships.

It was gone.

No blue lights left on the board.

Not a one.

Just Seeder green lights and hundreds of millions of alien red lights.

"*Star Rain,* what happened to The Creators' ships?" Benny asked.

"The entire fleet of Creators' ships," *Star Rain* said, "ran into an empty space pocket about twice the size of the empty space pocket that held the *Dreaming Large.*"

Benny just started laughing.

And after a moment most of the command center crew laughed with him.

Irony was a bitch, that was for sure.

TWELVE

GINA FOUND the meeting with the other four mission command chairmen and Ray and Tacita and Chairman West fun and somewhat funny. All of them thought the fact that The Creators' ships had run into an empty space bubble just laughable.

They were all in the *Star Mist* meeting room, as normal. Everyone in the room was dressed casually in jeans, light shirts, and tennis shoes except for Ray and Tacita. Both of them were in their standard black silk.

As far as Gina could tell through the laughter, the consensus of the nine was to leave The Creators' fleet in the bubble. The idiot Creators wouldn't even know any time had passed for a hundred thousand years or so.

After some laughing, a wonderful relief for these meetings, it was Matt who finally pointed out that their method of destroying entire galaxies of aliens was helping a little, even though none of them in the room agreed or liked The Creators' method.

Or liked the fact that they had caused all this in the first place, but Gina didn't say that. She knew they were all thinking it, though.

Ray nodded. "Our simulations show that given enough time, having The Creators and The Exterminators doing what they are doing might be the difference in the final outcome."

"A very slight difference," Tacita said.

Gina could tell that Tacita was just disgusted at The Creators and had no intention of hiding it.

Gina hated to admit that she agreed with that feeling.

"So are you suggesting we let those idiots out of there?" Benny asked.

Gina could tell from Benny's voice that he was surprised at the idea.

"Actually," West said, "It might be a great experiment for us to free them and get more data at the same time. It has been a very long time since we freed the *Dreaming Large.*"

Gina nodded to that. Anything at all that would speed up the development of control over empty-space bubbles would be a good thing. Even letting the idiots who caused this entire fight free again.

Ray nodded as well, but Tacita just looked more disgusted.

"Could we free them and not have them spot us?" Matt asked.

Ray and West both shook their heads.

"I'm afraid that wouldn't be possible," West said. "We would need to surround the bubble and their fleet and they would see us instantly when the bubble dropped."

"So we leave them," Angie said, "or rescue them and tell them we are here trying to clean up their mess."

"Pretty much those two options," Ray said.

"If they have to see us," Gage said, "at least can we direct them toward some alien galaxies that their destruction tactics would make more sense against?"

"That would help," Ray said, nodding.

Gina wasn't sure, but she thought she heard Tacita snort softly.

"So," Carrie said, "it seems pretty clear that none of us really want to free those idiots. Correct?"

Gina looked around and everyone was nodding, including Ray. Tacita's head was almost bobbing, she was nodding so hard.

"But," Carrie said, "it would give us a bubble release to study for West and his team if we freed them."

West nodded. "A very good example, actually."

"And," Carrie said, "in the long run of the war, if we directed them, they might be able to help in a slight way with the overall outcome. Do I have all that correct?"

Everyone nodded again.

Since it was the six of them running this entire operation, even though Ray and Tacita and West and numbers of other chairmen with ships now in the fight had seniority, only the six of them voted on any major decision.

And lately it had been Gina who had polled the six of them. She never polled unless she was sure of the outcome and right now she was sure. They had no other choice that she could see if they hoped to win this war.

"Angie?" Gina said.

"We release them."

"Gage?"

He nodded and shrugged. "Makes sense to release them."

"Carrie?" Gina asked.

Gina could tell that Carrie wanted no part of this vote, but she finally glanced at Matt and then said, "Release them."

"I agree," Matt said.

Gina looked at Benny and smiled. "Well?"

"Can we put them back into a bubble when this is all over?" Benny asked.

Gina and everyone laughed, and West said, "We get control of the empty space bubbles, I think that could be arranged without them even realizing they were in one."

"Then we release them for now," Benny said.

"I agree," Gina said, laughing. "For now."

"I think after the mess they have caused," Tacita said, "an empty space bubble is where they eventually belong."

Ray nodded to that and everyone else laughed.

THIRTEEN

"HAVE I SAID how much I hate this?" Benny asked as he stood next to Gina in their command center.

On the big screen was showing fifty small Seeder ships and *Rescue One*, Chairman West's ship. They were stationed at regular intervals in a globe form and Benny knew that in that globe shape was an empty space bubble holding an entire fleet of ships. The bubble was about ten times larger than a normal-sized solar system.

"Over the last six months?" Gina said, laughing, "I could have *Star Rain* count the times you have said that, because the number is far too big for me."

Benny shook his head and stared at the screen. "I don't care, I still hate this."

They had moved *Star Rain* to a position near the empty-space bubble holding The Creators' fleet. And when the fleet appeared after West and his people shut down the bubble, it was up to Benny and Gina to explain what had happened and what was going on in the battle against the aliens.

At first Benny thought it would be better to have Ray and Tacita talk with these people, since they were the ones that had sent them off into space to keep humanity safe. But both Ray and Tacita said there would be no point in bringing up old fights.

Million-year-old fights.

Benny thought that too stupid for words, but since The Creators were blowing up galaxies worth of planets in Benny and Gina's area of defense, it fell to them to do the meet and greet.

"Here we go," Chairman West said. "All systems show green. Everyone stand ready."

Benny and Gina turned and sat in their command chairs and *Star Rain* took over feeding them information across their screens. The Creators were going to be in for a shock since *Star Rain* was about four times the size of The Creators' biggest mother ship.

And when the ships were free, *Rescue One* and all of the smaller ships would jump to the new trans-tunnel flight and just vanish as far as The Creators' sensors would know.

"Permission to go?" Chairman West asked Benny and Gina.

Benny glanced at Gina and she nodded.

"Go," Benny said.

"*Star Rain*," Benny said, "stand ready to get us out of here instantly at any sign of trouble."

"Understood," *Star Rain* said.

"Mission is a go," Chairman West said.

A moment later an invisible bubble lit up as hundreds of thousands of small explosions spaced evenly around the empty space bubble punctured a hole in the gravitational membrane.

A moment later The Creators' fleet appeared.

West and his smaller ships vanished, leaving only *Star Rain* facing the fleet.

Benny studied the ships.

Seven-hundred-plus small ships, and all of them looked well-used. Four larger ships, three that he knew were nothing more than factory ships to build the explosives to blow up planets and build more small ships. The largest ship was the lead mother ship.

Luckily there were no alien ships also trapped in this bubble. Benny and Gina had a few dozen Sharks standing off ready in case there had been.

The Creators' fleet floated in space.

Benny and Gina just sat there, waiting.

From the perspective of The Creators' fleet, their trans-tunnels drives had suddenly shut down, then a moment later fifty ships surrounded them and then vanished, leaving only one big ship.

Six months had passed since the fleet had gone into the bubble, but to them it had only been a few seconds at most. So Benny and Gina were under no illusion that this was going to be a very interesting meeting.

"We are being hailed by the mother ship *Stahl*," *Star Rain* said.

"On our screens and the main screen," Gina said.

"Language translation complete," *Star Rain* said. "You will be speaking the language on the ship you are talking with."

"Thank you, *Star Rain*," Gina said.

An instant later a woman who looked to be about thirty, as all Seeders looked, appeared. She had dark brown hair chopped short and dark brown eyes. Her nose was long and her eyes set slightly too close together.

Benny and Gina had their image sent to her as well.

"I am Chairman Havemann of the mother ship *Stahl*," she said. "May I inquire as to what just happened and who you might be?"

Benny and Gina had decided that if the captain was a man, he would talk, if a woman, Gina would talk.

"Chairmen Slade and Helm of the Seeder mother ship *Star Rain*," Gina said. "You and your fleet were trapped for the last six months in an empty-space bubble. We just freed you."

"Six months?" Havemann asked.

She glanced around and clearly someone behind her confirmed that six months of time had passed. She turned back and Benny almost laughed at how her face had gone pale.

"I owe you our thanks," she said, bowing slightly.

Benny was surprised. From what Ray and Tacita had said, he did not expect any kind of courtesy or respect from anyone in this fleet

"You are more than welcome," Gina said.

Benny could tell that Gina was surprised as well at the courtesy.

"You are Seeder?" Havemann said. "We only know of you as ancient myth."

That surprised Benny as well, but Ray and Tacita had warned them that might be the case.

"None of your original Creators remain?" Gina asked, her voice level.

Havemann frowned. "I do not understand why you would call us Creators?"

"Didn't you create this race you are trying to stop?" Gina asked.

"We did that," Havemann said, nodding with a sad look on her face. "Our ancestors over four hundred generations removed let an experiment get out of hand and we have spent every moment since trying to stop the expansion of the experiment."

Benny opened his mouth to say something, but Gina squeezed his hand and he didn't say a word. It was clear to him that these Creators did not live long lifespans like normal Seeders.

In fact, from his quick math of the time since the alien expansion started, these ships were full of just regular life-span humans.

That was something Ray and Tacita had not warned them about. It seemed that the Seeder long-life gene was very rare and was not passed down or activated on these Creators' ships over the millions of years.

So everyone on the ships had been born on the ships and would die on the ships. They had been fighting these aliens for four hundred plus generations.

Benny just felt stunned at that thought. The Creators were humans, not Seeders.

FOURTEEN

GINA WAS DOING her best to maintain a calm, collected outer face when talking with Chairman Havemann, but she knew she needed to collect herself a little more and talk with the other chairmen before going on. This meeting was not at all what she had expected.

"Do you have the history of your voyage in space?" Gina asked.

Chairman Havemann shook her head. "We do not. The first part and why we were in space in the first place was lost right after what is known as the 'awakening.' We do not honestly know what that even means."

Gina had a hunch she knew and right now she really, really needed to have a few words with Ray and Tacita.

Maybe forceful words.

Gina smiled at Chairman Havemann. "May I beg your indulgence and ask for a short break. It will give you time to make sure your fleet is fully functional and allow me to consult with others as to what information we can give you."

Chairman Havemann looked puzzled, but nodded. "Of course."

"Thank you," Gina said and cut the connection.

"What the hell is going on?" Benny asked as they both stood.

"That's exactly what we need to find out," Gina said. "*Star Rain,* please ask the other chairmen for an emergency meeting on *Star Mist* and include Chairmen Ray and Tacita."

"They have agreed," *Star Rain* said a moment later.

Gina took Benny's hand and a moment later they were in the *Star Mist* conference room. Gina knew that the other chairmen and Ray and Tacita had listened to the meeting.

Ray and Tacita were sitting at their end of the table when Benny and Gina appeared.

A second later the other four chairmen appeared as well.

"So what didn't you think to tell us about The Creators, as you called them?" Gina asked, not even trying to keep the anger out of her voice.

"What did you do to sabotage their ship?" Benny asked.

Gage was still standing as well. "That's why you were surprised that they were here. You didn't expect them to live much longer after they awoke, did you?"

"We did not," Tacita said, her voice as cold and low as Gina had ever heard it. "And these aliens we are fighting that they created is the reason we tried to do what we did."

"And we succeeded," Ray said. "In what we tried."

"We should have blown their ships out of space," Tacita said.

Gina just shook her head, ignoring the anger coming from Tacita. "You sabotaged their ship to destroy their records after they awoke, right?"

"We did," Ray said, nodding.

"And you made sure their Seeder genes would go dormant while they slept, correct?" Gage asked.

"We did," Ray said, nodding. "We expected them to settle on a planet and just go from there. It felt like a humane thing to do and still stop their mission."

"We never expected them to continue on in space," Tacita said.

"That was why when we realized who they were," Ray said, "we assumed our attempt at sabotaging their Seeder genes

had failed and that many of the original crew would be still alive."

"That was why we did not want to talk with them," Tacita said. "Or even contact them. We held nothing back from you."

"We had no idea we had succeeded," Ray said. "Yet failed to stop them at the same time."

"The fact that hundreds and thousands of generations would have stayed on those ships never occurred to us," Tacita said. "Otherwise we would have told you that was possible."

"What about The Exterminators' fleet?" Gage asked.

"We did the same with them," Tacita said.

"We could take no chances that something like this might happen," Ray said.

"In that we failed," Tacita said.

Ray nodded and both of them looked down at the table.

Gina just felt washed out.

She dropped into a chair and Benny sat down hard beside her.

How stupid was this? They now had two fleets of humans flying from galaxy to galaxy destroying millions of alien-rat-infested planets.

What the hell could she even tell the humans?

Beside her Benny looked around at the chairmen in the room. "That fleet of humans, who are doing nothing more than trying to clean up a mess their distant ancestors caused, will need some sort of answers. Anyone have any bright ideas?"

Gina glanced around the room at all the shaking heads.

Great.

Just great.

FIFTEEN

THE EIGHT CHAIRMEN talked for over a half hour before finally deciding to do nothing for now.

Benny felt disgusted about that, but at least he won on giving the human ships, both fleets, better information. And telling them that the Seeders were also fighting to stop the aliens.

Everyone agreed that should be done.

He and Gina returned to *Star Rain* and got into their command chair. Then they had *Star Rain* contact Chairman Havemann again.

Benny had promised Gina he would try to keep his mouth shut. He had no doubt that was going to be difficult at best.

"Sorry for the interruption, Chairman" Gina said. "We had to consult with others before moving forward."

Chairman Havemann nodded, clearly puzzled, but said nothing.

"We are from a branch of humans called Seeders," Gina said. "Our ship and many others are here from occupied human galaxies to try to stop these aliens your ancestors created."

"Occupied human galaxies?" Havemann asked, looking puzzled.

"Humans fill many millions of galaxies now," Gina said.

Benny was shocked. For a moment he thought Chairman Havemann might break down right there. But somehow the Chairman held it together. But clearly what Gina had said went against much of what those on the ships had learned over the centuries.

"We believed the two fleets were alone in space," she said. "And we have been unable to find a planet over centuries that we wanted to settle."

"You are far from alone," Gina said. "Right now we have over sixty thousand Seeder ships here fighting the alien expansion, with more coming every month from human galaxies."

"How far is the nearest human galaxy?" Havemann asked, almost breathless.

Benny felt bad. This poor woman and the millions who followed her were doing their best.

"It would take your fleet two-hundred-thousand years to make the journey," Gina said.

"Oh," Havemann said.

Benny felt very bad for Havemann at that point. To a human with a normal life-span, as he thought he had not that many years before, two-hundred-thousand years was difficult to even imagine.

Hell, he couldn't imagine it yet.

"We can discuss all that later," Gina said, moving on. "But right now we need you and your fleet to continue what you are doing. But we can help you pinpoint galaxies in early alien growth instead of later alien growth."

Chairman Havemann nodded.

Benny could see her doing her best to focus back on the task at hand.

"That would help all our morale," Chairman Havemann said.

"My ship is sending you now the next five galaxies you are close to that we need you to take care of," Gina said. "We have decided to fight the alien ships as they leave galaxies."

"Are you in contact with the other fleet?" Chairman Havemann asked.

"We are not," Gina said. "Are you?"

"Yes, we are working together as best we could over such vast distances. They were very worried at our sudden silence for six months."

"My ship is sending you the data of galaxies the other fleet can attack to be more helpful," Gina said. "Please relay the information to them."

Chairman Havemann nodded. "I will."

"Thank you," Gina said. "We will be in regular contact and update you on the status of the battle as it goes on."

"You clearly can see a bigger picture than we can," Havemann said, looking first at Gina, then at Benny.

Benny, with that one look, could see why this woman was the leader of her fleet. She was intense and very smart.

Gina nodded.

"What is the status of stopping the alien expansion?" Havemann asked.

"We are losing," Gina said.

Benny would have tried to say that in a less-blunt fashion.

Havemann nodded.

Benny didn't think she seemed surprised.

"But we have a lot more help on the way," Gina said. "Given time we will wipe your ancestors' experiment from the stars."

"Thank you for that," Havemann said. "Please allow us to help in any fashion we can."

Gina nodded. "For now, continue onward. That's all any of us can do."

"Thank you for the rescue," Havemann said. "And for letting us know you are here with us."

"We will be in touch again soon," Gina said, nodding.

She cut the connection.

Then Gina said to *Star Rain,* "Jump us out of here and back to our home position."

Benny glanced at Gina. He could tell she was very, very upset.

And Benny wasn't feeling that happy either. A group of humans were fighting an impossible fight against all odds to fix a mistake that distant ancestors had made and stupid politics from millions of years before blocked the Seeder's ships from helping them in any real way.

If Benny had anything to say about that, that million-year-old stupid policy was going to change and change soon.

And as upset as Gina felt beside him, that change would happen sooner rather than later.

And maybe then, just maybe, those millions of humans in that fleet and the second fleet might actually get a chance to stop.

But first, there was a war to win.

SECTION FOUR
Even More Help

SIXTEEN

GINA LOVED HOW sometimes Benny's thinking would show them ways of doing things they had not thought about before. But more often than not, he just pointed out a missing problem they had to deal with.

The year after they had saved the human fleet from the empty space, Benny and Gina were reading morning reports while in their command chair. Benny had cooked them both a wonderful cheese omelet for breakfast and both had spent an hour exercising.

For the past year, more and more fighting help had poured into the battle from human occupied parts of known space. But Gina and everyone knew they were still losing the overall fight.

And Gina saw no real chance that would change anytime into the near future.

And so far there had been no real progress on the empty-space bubble research, although Chairman West of *Rescue One* reported the research was ramping up wonderfully.

Gina had become friends with Chairman Havemann of the human Creators fleet and had been helping them where she could. The more she got to know Havemann and the humans in that fleet, the more she had come to respect them, even though it was their ancestors who had started this entire mess.

Every month, Gina gave a report to the other chairmen about the human fleet, slowly swaying all of them to a position of willingness to help them.

The human fleet had changed course toward the new galaxy Gina and the Seeders had suggested, and the human fleet was still fourteen years from reaching that target.

"Ever noticed how many alien ships just miss their target?" Benny asked, seemingly out of the blue.

Benny pointed out one alien ship on the report that had been spotted far outside the lines of defense. It had been lost and traveling for almost thirty thousand years. Its occupants were long dead, since the aliens had no way to save themselves when a ship malfunctioned.

Gina had only nodded to that, not really paying much attention, until Benny asked *Star Rain* a question.

"*Star Rain,* would it be possible to estimate how many alien ships miss their target?"

"It would be possible," *Star Rain* said.

Gina looked at her partner and the man she loved more than she could ever love another person. Benny was just nodding. She wasn't sure where he was headed with this sort of questioning.

"*Star Rain,*" he said, "with the information we now have about alien ships, how long could the aliens on a ship survive in space without finding a new planet?"

"Extreme outside limit would be one-hundred-thousand years," *Star Rain* said. "The occupants of the ship found near the Milky Way galaxy had survived almost that long."

"Logical amount of time," Benny asked.

"It would be unlikely," *Star Rain* said, "for the alien occupants to survive beyond twenty-thousand years. Most would not make it that long."

Gina still wasn't certain why Benny was asking these questions, but she let him go. She had learned early on in their relationship that when he had his mind on a line of thought, it was better to let him just run down the line to the end.

"Wow," Benny said to himself, shaking his head. "*Star Rain,* would you have an estimation of a failure rate of the alien ships?"

"The construction of the aliens ships is so basic in its nature," *Star Rain* said, "the failure rate is very low. Estimated at less than one-hundredth of a percent."

Gina felt suddenly very thankful for that, since once an alien ship found a planet, it was not used again. The aliens were not able to continue to reuse old ships, they only knew how to build new ones.

"*Star Rain,* since the start of the alien expansion," Benny said, "taking into account the increased numbers of alien ships as time went on the best you can, would you give a general, and I understand rough, estimate of the number of alien ships that have malfunctioned."

"The number," *Star Rain* said, "using every guideline we know to this point about alien ships, would be approximately two-hundred-million alien-ship failures."

Gina just shook her head. Nothing about this battle ever seemed to work out in small numbers. But she still wasn't sure where Benny was going with this line of questions, so she kept quiet.

"*Star Rain,*" Benny said, "I am assuming many of those failures would be in the lifting from a planet's gravity well, other failures would be in trying to land on a new planet. Am I correct in assuming such a thing?"

"Yes," *Star Rain* said. "Almost all failures would occur on the alien ship's attempt at landing on a destination planet."

"Over the entire time of alien expansion, would you estimate how many alien-ship failures would cause them to miss the galaxy they were aiming at, as the alien ship did that was found near the Milky Way?"

"Under one-hundred thousand," *Star Rain* said.

Gina felt her stomach twist up into a knot. Now she understood exactly what Benny was trying to find out. The dead alien ship that had been reported today would have been one of those ships.

"How likely would it be for one of those ships," Benny asked *Star Rain,* "with navigation malfunction, to safely land on a planet in another galaxy?"

"Extremely unlikely," *Star Rain* said.

Three Cold Poker Gang Novels
Available at your favorite booksellers.

"But still possible?"

"Yes," *Star Rain* said.

"Shit," Gina said softly.

"I'm going to need to see this on the big display," Benny said, squeezing Gina's hand and standing.

Gina stood with him.

Behind them the command center just functioned in its normal soft talk among a few of the crew.

"*Star Rain*," Benny said, "please show an image of the known universe within a twenty-thousand-year standard trans-tunnel drive diameter from the alien expansion start as the center. Please figure in the years since the start of that expansion."

A massive cloud of white dots filled the air above Gina. Each dot was a galaxy.

Behind her all movement and talking of the command crew stopped.

"All it would take would be one ship," Benny said softly.

Gina stared at the massive cloud of a billion galaxies. She needed to ask yet another question.

"*Star Rain*, would it be possible to narrow down likely alien infestation areas from what we know of the alien expansion patterns from each galaxy? If so, please show us those."

Huge amounts of the vast cloud of galaxies vanished, leaving what looked like spokes of a wheel radiating from this area of space.

Twenty spokes, twenty major paths likely taken by malfunctioning alien ships.

"Is it likely that a malfunctioning alien ship found a new planet along one of those paths?" Benny asked.

"No, not likely," *Star Rain* said. "Thirty decimal places below one percent chance."

"But possible?" Gina asked.

"Yes," *Star Rain* said.

Behind Gina she could tell a few of the command crew had picked up on the problem by soft swear words or a slight gasp.

"Ahh, the fun just continues," Benny said, shaking his head.

All Gina could do was stare at the millions of possible galaxies in the star cloud in front of her that might already be infected with aliens.

She didn't consider any of this fun.

SEVENTEEN

BENNY KNEW WHAT they had to do after his little question and answer session with *Star Rain*. They needed, without delay, to send out small fleets of ships along those spoke lines, spread out enough and with the new long-range sensors, to look for alien ships that had missed and were out there.

And those ships along the way needed to pop every empty space bubble they came across to make sure no alien ship was lurking like a bad bomb in one of them.

Given enough time and enough firepower and a lot of luck, Benny believed the aliens could be contained and then destroyed in this area of space.

But if one alien ship got out, found a new planet to infest, and was spreading out there somewhere, that infestation needed to be found and stopped.

He presented his thinking to the other chairmen on the same afternoon. All agreed with him. And left it to him and Gina to pick the form of the fleets and the head of each fleet.

Benny figured each fleet could consist of one military mother ship capable of holding five hundred of the ten-man Sharks.

With the Sharks spread out, they could scan a vast amount of space along the likely trails of alien ships. And there would be enough ships to rotate back into the mother ship regularly.

Gina really liked that plan and so did the other chairmen.

The alien ships would take thirty thousand years to travel a certain distance, but with the new trans-tunnel drive, the small military fleet could make the same journey in less than a year.

So Benny and Gina figured they only needed five fleets and could get the job mostly done in less than ten years.

Even Ray and Tacita thought the idea worth the ships and the time.

So only one month after Benny came up with the idea, he and Gina wished Chairman June of the military mother ship *Deep Cycle* good hunting.

The other five fleets left over the next three months.

And except for the weekly reports all the chairmen got, Benny thought nothing much more about those small fleets for the next eleven months. The fleets had found and destroyed a number of stray ships under power, and found no infestations at all along the way.

And they had popped thousands and thousands of the empty-space bubbles without finding a ship either.

But eleven months and six days after *Deep Cycle* left, Benny and Gina got an emergency message from Chairman June.

Chairman Constance June was a bright-eyed woman with long red hair, white skin with freckles, and a biting sense of humor that Benny liked.

Benny and Gina sat in their command chair and told *Star Rain* to keep the communication private for the moment.

Chairman June's face appeared and Benny was shocked. The woman seemed to have not slept in a very long time from the looks of her eyes and her hair had come loose from how she normally tied it back from her face.

"Chairman," Gina said, "what happened?"

"We found an infestation," Chairman June said. "At this point it's held to about fifty galaxies as far as we can tell."

Benny just shook his head. Exactly what he had been afraid of.

Exactly.

"Oh, no," Gina said. Then she said, "Chairman, please send all your data to *Star Rain* now."

Chairman June turned and nodded.

A moment later *Star Rain* said, "I have received the data."

"Is the infestation containable?" Benny asked *Star Rain*.

"It is," *Star Rain* said.

"Containing is not the issue," Chairman June said. "Take a look at this."

Replacing Chairman June's face an image appeared.

The image was of an alien ship powering through deep space between galaxies. Then another ship with a slightly saucer shape and what almost looked like a tail, like a sting-ray in an ocean, came in from the side and with one shot destroyed the alien ship.

If Benny hadn't been firmly held with the form-fitting command chair, he would have gone over backwards.

"What the hell was that?" Benny asked.

"Another group fighting the alien infestation," Chairman June said.

"Humans?" Gina asked.

Chairman June shook her head.

Benny could see the Chairman was almost in shock. "They have a slight humanoid shape, large heads, no nose or ears, large eyes, and are very short and thin."

A moment later a picture of the new alien appeared on the screen.

Chairman June had been correct. Huge head, large round eyes, triangle-shaped head.

Benny didn't find them repulsive as he had some aliens found over the millions of years by Seeder scout ships. Nothing at all like the rat-like aliens they were fighting.

"Not possible," Gina said. "Those are called the Grays on my home planet."

"Mine as well," Chairman June said.

And suddenly Benny realized where he had seen images of these aliens. On television, back on Earth, before the Event destroyed most everything. They had supposedly visited Earth or something like that. He had never paid much attention to that sort of stuff.

Now he wished he had.

Who knew he was going to need it?

EIGHTEEN

GINA FORCED HERSELF to take a deep breath and think.

What they had discovered wasn't possible by all Seeder records, yet it was happening. The Grays were seemingly fighting an infestation of the aliens.

"Do the Grays know you are there?"

Chairman June shook her head. "We have remained shielded and all Sharks have pulled back inside."

"Good thinking," Benny said. "What kind of capability do the Gray ships have?"

"They have standard trans-tunnel drive is all, but they seemed to be able to pinpoint alien ships, so they must have decent scanners," Captain June said. "They are using the same strategy we are using in letting the aliens have a galaxy once infested, but destroying any alien ship that leaves the galaxy."

Gina was glad to hear that at least.

"Could you tell the size of their fleet?" Benny asked.

"A half-million ships approximately," Chairman June said. "And more seem to be coming from the direction on the other side of this alien infestation."

"Do they seem to be winning against the aliens?" Gina asked.

"Our calculations show that they are not," Chairman June said.

"Star Rain?" Benny asked. "From the data sent to you, are the Grays winning against the alien infestation?"

Chairman June is correct," *Star Rain* said. "The Grays stand a zero percent chance against the alien infestation."

"Yet we can defeat it?" Gina asked.

"We can," *Star Rain* said.

Gina glanced at Benny who looked at her and nodded.

"Chairman June," Gina said. "Please hold your position and continue to feed *Star Rain* information as you get it."

Chairman June nodded.

"We will be back to you shortly."

Chairman June's face vanished to be replaced with an image of the new alien infestation. Compared to what they were fighting here, it was very small.

"Star Rain," Gina said, "please contact *Star Mist* and *Star Fall* and ask for an emergency meeting."

"Also invite Chairman Ray and Tacita," Benny said.

Benny and Gina both stood.

"They have agreed," *Star Rain* said a moment later.

"I need to find something out before this meeting," Benny said to Gina.

Benny turned to the thirty friends that was their command crew. He had come to know and respect and trust all of them.

"Honest show of hands," Benny said, "how many of you on your home worlds heard of aliens called the Grays with big heads and big eyes?"

About three quarters of the command crew raised their hands and then looked at the others around them, surprised.

Benny just shook his head. "There is something very fishy going on. What smells like fish, looks like fish, and tastes like fish, must be fish."

Gina just shook her head. "Want to bet it's just another part of history no one bothered to tell us about."

"No damn bet," Benny said.

NINETEEN

BENNY WAS GETTING damn tired of not being told things and being fed history in bits and pieces like a kid who didn't really need to know things. That just made running a massive war like this dangerous.

If the Grays were spotted on so many human planets in so many different galaxies, it was clear there was much more to their presence here than met the eye.

When Benny and Gina arrived in the conference room, Angie and Gage were already in their chairs, as were Ray and Tacita. Carrie and Matt were just pulling out their chairs.

"So we got a fun report from Chairman June of the *Deep Cycle*," Benny said as he and Gina sat down. "Seems they found an alien infestation."

Benny decided he wanted to see what kind of reaction he was going to get from Ray and Tacita.

"Oh, shit," Gage said, sitting forward.

"What we were worried about," Gina said, nodding. "Spread to about fifty galaxies and *Star Rain* tells us we can contain it from the data Chairman June sent us."

"Good," Ray said, nodding.

Benny watched as everyone nodded, clearly surprised at the news, but relieved at the fact that the outbreak could be contained.

"But we have one interesting problem," Gina said.

Benny laughed, pretending he wasn't really annoyed. "Interesting describes it. Seems the outbreak is already being fought by the Grays."

Tacita actually jerked and Ray sat back, clearly shocked. In fact, for as old as those two were, that statement rocked them more than Benny had seen them rocked before.

"Grays?" Gage said.

"Are you talking about the mythical aliens that supposedly visited our Earth?" Angie asked. "The ones with the big heads, big eyes, and little tiny bodies?"

"One and the same," Benny said, nodding.

"We polled our command crew and three quarters of them, from many different galaxies, had heard rumors of the Grays."

"What the hell?" Matt asked, turning to look at Ray and Tacita.

"Now what haven't you told us?" Gage asked.

"I'm sick and tired of being kept in the dark all the time," Angie said, staring at Ray and Tacita.

Benny wasn't surprised at the anger. He was feeling it as well.

Ray and Tacita just sat there, shaking their heads. Both of them were a long way from their eyes.

Finally Ray sort of took a deep breath and looked at Tacita. "A fleet of them must have followed The Creators and The Exterminators."

Tacita nodded. "It would be the only explanation."

"How many ships do they have in the fight?" Ray asked.

"Estimated at about a half million with more coming from the other side of the infestation," Benny said.

That wouldn't be a group just following them," Ray said, clearly puzzled. "This must be closer to their home space."

Benny didn't much like the sound of that at all.

"Ships like saucers with tails?" Tacita asked.

"Yes," Benny said. Then he said simply, "We're all just sitting here waiting for an explanation and why we were never told of these aliens? We were always told there were no other galaxy-spanning race but humans out here."

Ray looked at Tacita and she shrugged.

"We had a treaty with the Grays," Ray said, turning to face the six angry chairmen. "We would wipe their presence from our history, tell no one of their existence, and they would help us in our seeding of galaxies."

Benny glanced at Gina who just sat there clearly still angry.

"Back up to the start," Benny said. "But first, are you telling me that chairmen of mother ships don't even know about the Grays?"

"There are less than one hundred Seeders in all the known universe that know of their existence," Tacita said.

"It has been the best kept secret in all of humanities history," Ray said.

"Seems that secret has sort of hit the bright light of day now," Gage said.

Ray and Tacita said nothing.

"So why the big secret about this treaty?" Angie asked.

"Because it was the Grays that rescued us on the very first Earth from destroying ourselves," Tacita said softly.

Benny sat back so hard, the chair rocked.

"They helped us to survive," Ray said, "but then made us promise we would never help another alien race. It seems they looked on us as a mistake."

Benny wanted to say, You mean like the aliens we are fighting are a mistake. But he didn't.

TWENTY

THE SILENCE in the conference room felt like a thick cloud that made it hard to breathe. Gina pushed back from the table some and just forced herself to breathe.

Then she broke the silence with a question. "How much older are the Grays than humanity?"

"No one knows," Ray said. "They did not originate in our original galaxy, we do know that. They were only coming through when we were emerging from the original Earth."

"They may look slightly human-oid," Tacita said, "but they are a silica-based life form. They live in dry regions of Earth-like planets and underground in vast caverns, completely hidden from the world above them. Too much water is actually deadly to them."

"So that's why so many human cultures have seen them?" Angie asked.

Ray nodded. "When we first started terraforming planets, we worked with them to make sure, as best we could, that each planet was suitable for both human and Gray life."

"They didn't need that much space," Tacita said. "Just enough to house a few of what they call their hives."

"They have been expanding with humanities expansion?" Gage asked.

"Yes," Ray nodded. "But early on it became clear that humans were too fearful of the Grays, so the treaty was signed and the Grays have just kept themselves mostly hidden from the human populations on a planet."

"We honestly know very little about them beyond that," Tacita said.

"Have you ever met a Gray?" Benny asked before Gina could.

"Tacita and I negotiated the treaty with them," Ray said.

"We have not talked to a member of their race since," Tacita said.

"With only one exception, no Seeder has talked to a member of their race in any capacity that we know of in millions of years," Ray said.

Silence filled the room and Gina welcomed it as all eight of them sat there, all clearly lost in thought.

So once again, information about the past of the Seeders and humanity had been held from them and now it was suddenly in play. For such a vast universe, it sure seemed to be suddenly damn small.

Gina could feel her anger draining away. Ray and Tacita would have no reason to tell them of the Gray for this mission or for any mission, actually.

"So what do we do now?" Angie asked. "We have about forty thousand long-lived Seeders on *Deep Cycle* that now know about the Grays."

"Not counting our entire command crew," Gina said.

"And since the Grays are losing that fight," Benny said, "they are going to need the help from their mistake to defeat our mistake."

Gina laughed and the others just shook their heads and smiled.

"We will need to talk with the Grays," Tacita said, glancing at Ray.

He nodded. "This is not a secret we can keep any longer among Seeders. We must continue to keep it from the general human populations on planets."

"It seems that Seeders keep a lot of secrets," Gina said. "So that shouldn't be so hard."

"Agreed," Carrie said.

The other chairmen nodded.

Gina looked at Benny and he nodded, as if he could read her mind.

She turned to Ray and Tacita. "I would suggest that we move *Star Rain* to the new infestation until we have it contained. *Star Mist* and *Star Fall* can continue to direct the fight in this area."

Ray and Tacita made no move at all, but the other chairmen nodded.

"The aliens are our mess," Benny said. "If the Gray want to continue to help, fine. But they are losing and we need to stop this infestation quickly while it is manageable. We don't have time for million-year-old politics."

"You put our three ships and the six of us in charge of this battle for a reason," Gina said, staring at Ray and Tacita. "Now let us do our jobs."

Ray nodded to that.

Gina watched as Tacita sat dead still, no expression on her face at all.

"The six of us will have you an infestation containment plan in three days," Benny said to Ray and Tacita. "One with the Grays helping and one with the Grays pulling back."

"We will need to talk with the Grays and explain the situation," Ray said.

"I see no reason, since you negotiated the old treaty, why you would not remain the contact person with them," Gage said.

Gina nodded and noticed everyone else did the same.

"Star Mist," Angie said into the air, "what are the chances at this point we will defeat the aliens and stop them from spreading through known space?"

"With the forces we have or could bring to bear by a likely foreseeable future point," Star Mist said, "the aliens will not be contained. So there is zero percent chance of containment, to answer your question directly."

"Thank you, Star Mist," Angie said.

Then Gina watched as Angie turned back to Ray and Tacita.

"You need to do more than explain to them the problem," Angie said. "You need to get them to help us. They live on worlds that will be destroyed by the aliens as well."

Ray nodded. "I do not think the Grays know we are here or where these aliens came from."

"Oh, that's going to be a fun conversation," Benny said.

"Just get them to help," Benny said. "Even it means giving them the technology for the faster trans-tunnel drive."

Ray and Tacita's heads both snapped around to look at Gina and Benny.

Gina was shocked at that reaction.

"Are you saying they only have standard trans-tunnel drive?" Ray asked.

"That's how their ships are moving," Benny said, "from the first reports from Deep Cycle."

Ray turned to look at Tacita. She was looking slightly shocked.

Gina had no idea why.

Ray turned back to look at Gina and Benny. "Do not bother with a battle plan where the Grays do not help."

Tacita nodded at that.

Then both of them stood.

"We must consult with a few others who know of and study the Grays," Ray said.

"Please, please," Angie said, "keep us informed on what you find."

Tacita nodded to that. "We will. This secret is now past a point of value."

"And please move Star Rain toward the new infestation at highest possible speed," Ray said. "Negotiating with the Grays from a position of power on a huge mother ship will be helpful."

Gina understood that completely.

A moment later Ray and Tacita were gone.

The six of them just sat there.

Finally Benny said, "Well, can't say this job is boring."

Gina could only laugh at that.

TWENTY-ONE

SIX MONTHS LATER, completely shielded and with a force of eighty military mother ships on board and thousands and thousands of the small attack ships called Sharks, *Star Rain* eased into position near *Deep Cycle.*

Benny had been studying the battle the Grays had been fighting against the aliens and it had become clear that their long-range scanners were not that good. Some alien ships were getting through.

So the chairmen had authorized the Sharks on *Deep Cycle* to take care of the alien ships that had gotten through while staying shielded. That way they didn't give some of those alien ships a six-month free pass.

During that six months, thousands more Gray ships had poured into the area. But the Grays still had no hope of containing this infestation with their slower ships and scanning that wasn't picking up all alien ships.

Ray and Tacita had kept their promise and kept the chairmen informed about what they found from research with those who had more knowledge about the Grays. It seemed that it was always rumored that the Grays had a large region of space and occupied planets in hundreds of thousands of galaxies.

It was also clear that they did not much care for humans, but tolerated them. When on human planets that Seeders had altered and planted human populations, the Grays stayed completely hidden and shielded from the humans and liked it that way.

Benny had suggested that *Star Rain* launch all its ships and *Deep Cycle* do the same and all drop shields at the same time as Ray and Tacita moved to contact the Grays. It would be an impressive show of power and force.

Ray and Tacita both agreed.

It took almost a full day for *Star Rain* and *Deep Cycle* to launch all the ships they had been carrying and spread them out into a formation behind them facing the battle galaxies that would look impressive. The formation covered almost two light years.

And each ship had a destination area planned in the battle and locked in when *Star Rain* gave the go-ahead.

Again Benny was stunned at the scale that Seeders just worked naturally.

Then Ray and Tacita jumped to the Command Center of *Star Rain.*

Everyone in the room bowed slightly when they appeared and dead silence filled the massive space.

It dawned on Benny that his command crew had never had a chance to meet the legendary Chairmen Ray and Tacita. After the last decades, he had forgotten they were special.

Gina stood beside Benny on his right and Ray and Tacita stood beside him to the left.

"Ready?" Benny asked.

Both Ray and Tacita nodded.

"Not a word, folks," Benny said, turning to look at the command crew behind him. "Not even a slight noise. And bow when we bow."

He got nods as he turned back.

"*Star Rain,*" Benny said, "Have all ships drop shields on my mark."

"Standing by," *Star Rain* said.

"Now," Benny said.

On one part of the big screen it showed the image of the massive Seeders fleet spread over a large area of space. The military mother ships were slightly in front of their vast numbers of Sharks.

Star Rain led the large fleet and *Deep Cycle* was second and back, showing which ship was in command clearly.

The Gray fleet could now suddenly see the Seeders' fleet. That was going to be a shock, Benny figured.

"Seeders Chairmen Ray and Tacita to talk with the honored Grays fleet commander," Ray said.

Benny knew Ray's words were translated into the language of the Grays and sent to all ships within fifty galaxies. He also knew that the image of the four of them standing and waiting was also being broadcast.

Ray had warned them to not be impatient, that it would take some time for the Grays commander to study the situation and respond. They were a methodical race.

So they all stood, hands behind their backs, staring at the screen in front of them.

It took almost four full minutes before the screen flickered and an image of a Gray appeared. Large head, large round eyes, thin neck and seemingly no clothes at all. Benny had no idea how they told each other apart, since every image Benny had seen of them seemed to be identical.

Ray, Tacita, Benny and Gina all bowed.

And Benny hoped like hell that everyone behind them bowed as well.

"Thank you for speaking with us, Great One," Ray said as he came up out of his bow.

The Gray bowed slightly in response. "It has been many millions of what you call year-cycles since our last conversation. I am honored."

What might have been considered the Gray's mouth did not really move as he spoke.

And clearly they knew Ray and Tacita just fine. And that meant that they either lived as long as Seeders or had a solid hive-mind memory.

"The honor is ours," Ray said. "I would request a private meeting to talk

about the situation we face with this dangerous and expanding alien race."

The Gray nodded just slightly. Then said, "It would seem to be in our mutual best interests."

"Thank you," Ray said, nodding.

"I am afraid all of our ships are military in nature and would not be suited for such a meeting," the Gray said. "So this meeting will need to take place in this communication mode if that is acceptable to you, Chairmen Ray and Tacita."

"Acceptable," Ray said, bowing.

Tacita nodded.

"Please take the time you need to prepare," Ray said. "But may I ask permission for our smaller ships to move out around the battle area and help in tracking down and destroying the alien ships while our discussion continues."

The Gray's expression did not change, but Benny would have bet anything it was puzzled.

Ray did not force the Gray to ask, but instead continued onward.

"Our ships are very fast," Ray said. "We can move between galaxies at less time than what we call a day in our time-cycle. And our scanning equipment can pinpoint an alien ship moving throughout this entire battle area from any location."

The Gray seemed to think for a moment, then nodded. "You have our permission. We will talk again in exactly two of your cycle days."

The screen went blank, replaced by the image of the huge battle area.

"*Star Rain*," Benny said, "have everyone scramble to assigned areas at top speed. Let's show the Grays what we can do in the next forty-eight hours."

"And that's exactly what we wanted," Ray said, nodding.

He glanced at Benny and Gina. "Thank you both. We will return before the next meeting."

And with that, Ray and Tacita jumped away.

"Well," Benny said, shaking his head and turning to face his command crew still looking shocked at their stations, "that was fun."

SECTION FIVE
The Price of Help

TWENTY-TWO

WITH BOTH THE Gray and the Seeders' fleets attacking the new infestation, it had become clear that this battle would be under control fairly quickly.

Gina liked that, like the feeling of actually accomplishing something after so much bad news.

Ray and Tacita had met with the Grays ten times over a period of two months and now, today, back in the conference room on *Star Mist,* they were going to detail out the talks and possible agreement.

Gina and Benny were already in their seats around the large conference table, as were Carrie and Matt and Angie and Gage, when Ray and Tacita arrived.

Gina looked for any sign they were tired or happy or anything, but the two just seemed to go through life on a very, very even level. After being alive for that many millions of years, Gina figured there wasn't that much that could shock them.

After Ray and Tacita were seated, Ray said, "We have come to an agreement with the Grays."

Gina and everyone just nodded.

"The terms are basic," Tacita said. "We will give them the improvements to the trans-tunnel flight in exchange for them sending a large fleet to help us contain this area."

Gina was very happy to hear that their numbers were going to be large enough.

"They will retrofit their military ships with the new drive and build more," Ray said. "They will, with the first fleet of their improved ships take over the defense of the infestation they were fighting."

"Our ships will be free to return at that point," Tacita said. "That timeline should be five years."

Gina nodded to that.

"The Grays believe that in ten years they could have five million of their ships fighting in this area," Ray said.

"Wow," Benny said.

Carrie and Gage smiled. Gina felt the same way. Five million more ships plus the million more Seeder ships being built in that period of time will give them a chance at holding the line against the alien ships.

"We have agreed," Tacita said, "to modify our original treaty so that Seeders can know about the Gray, but no human."

"That should protect their millions of cities on human planets," Ray said.

Gina liked that as well until Tacita said the next sentence.

"We must therefore," Tacita said, "remove the human Creators' fleet and the Exterminators' fleet from the fight before the first Gray ship shows up here in three years."

"And how do you intend to do that?" Angie asked a half second before Gina could.

"In six months the mother ship *Evening Tide* is scheduled to arrive here," Ray said. "Chairmen Leigh and Oliver have offered to unload the military ships they are bringing and take both fleets back about halfway to the human occupied sector and find them a suitable planet for a home base."

Gina nodded and the room was silent. Gina knew that *Evening Tide* could hold every ship in both human fleets without a problem.

"And if they don't want to go?" Benny asked.

"That will be up to you and Gina to make sure they agree," Ray said. "We have no choice. The Grays fighting with us on this will make the difference."

Angie laughed. "And you told the Grays who created the aliens, didn't you?"

"We did," Tacita said. "And said they are being dealt with."

"We fight their fight," Ray said, a hint of anger in his voice, "clean up their ancestor's mess, they get to start over and settle down in a galaxy all their own. It is the fairest deal we can offer them."

Gina just shook her head.

"Bad blood still flowing deep after millions of years," Matt said, clearly disgusted.

"We should have just left them in the empty-space bubble," Gage said.

Ray and Tacita said nothing to that.

TWENTY-THREE

BENNY AND GINA stood in front of their command chairs, watching the big screen as *Star Rain* made final approach to The Creators' fleet of ships. The fleet looked tired, even from a distance. It was only a matter of time before they would no longer be able to go on.

He didn't much like the solution that was required for the two human fleets, but it was better than anything he could come up with. And from what they had learned about the two fleets of humans, they had always hoped to find a good place to settle, but had yet to find anything suitable.

And then a few hundred thousand years, they had only fought to contain their ancestor's mistakes. So they had taken no time to look for a new home. With the aliens on the move, no new home would be safe.

But the Seeder scout ships had found a couple of planets in a galaxy about halfway back to human space that were perfect, one for the Creators, one for the Exterminators, and yet close enough the two cultures could work between systems in trade.

And the galaxy could be protected from the aliens.

It was an ideal solution and one he and Gina had to sell. There was no other choice.

With the Grays coming into the fight here, there was a slight chance the aliens could be stopped and defeated. And a slight chance was better than they had had for the last few decades.

"Holding position with The Creators' mother ship, *Stahl*," *Star Rain* said.

Benny glanced at Gina. She took a deep breath and nodded that she was ready.

"Drop shields and ask for a conference with Chairman Havemann," Benny said.

Benny and Gina had decided they needed to do this in person, so they were going to ask permission to go on board the *Stahl* as no one in that fleet could teleport since they were all human.

A moment later, Chairman Havemann appeared on the screen in front of them. Benny was shocked that the younger-looking woman they had met the first time was showing signs of aging and had a pretty good streak of gray in her hair now.

Havemann smiled and nodded. "Wonderful speaking with you again, Chairman," she said bowing slightly. "But I assume since you and your magnificent ship are here, there is a problem."

Benny and Gina both smiled at her and nodded.

"There is," Gina said. "Benny and I would like to ask permission to talk with you and your command crew in private on your ship if we could."

Havemann nodded, no longer smiling. "Give me fifteen minutes to set it up in a conference room and I will send the location."

"No need," Gina said. "We will just jump to your location when you give the okay."

Havemann shook her head. "You can do that?" Then she laughed and said, "Of course you can do that. Fifteen minutes."

"Thank you, Chairman," Gina said and cut the connection.

Benny shook his head and asked, "*Star Rain,* without your translation, will we be able to talk in person?"

"There has been no translation," *Star Rain* said. "You have been speaking their language when you need to."

Benny laughed and glanced around at the command crew, a few of who were nodding and smiling.

"It felt so normal," Gina said, shaking her head, "I didn't know that either."

Benny laughed. "Never too old to learn I guess."

"How old are you anyway?" Gina asked, smiling at Benny with that sly grin he loved.

He laughed. "Old enough to know better, Chairman."

Then he kissed her.

TWENTY-FOUR

GINA WASN'T SURPRISED at the slightly shabby feel to the conference room when they transported on board the *Stahl*. It had what looked to be old metal panels on the walls that were gray and carpet that looked worn and forgotten.

The table was a fake wood but was actually metal and the chairs were just simply folding chairs of some sort. The air had a faint stale smell to it as well, as if it had been used and recycled a few million times too many.

Chairman Havemann stepped forward and shook both their hands.

Gina had liked Chairman Havemann from the start and liked her even more in person. But Gina was surprised at how tiny Havemann was. If she stood four ten, that would be tall.

And the other two with her were also very, very short. Shorter than Havemann. To the humans, she and Benny must have appeared like giants. Clearly millions of years of hundreds of thousands of generations living on board a ship had made height something that wasn't required.

Havemann wore a dark blouse and dark slacks and no shoes. Her face looked even older in person. Clearly the stress of being the chairman was wearing on her quickly.

The other two also wore dark shirts and slacks and no shoes. Maybe shoes had also become something not needed in shipboard living. Or they were just too much use of resources to be of value. Gina bet it was the latter.

Havemann introduced the two men with her as her first officers, one military, the other construction and operational. Both were older than Havemann looked and both clearly were shocked at the size and height of she and Benny.

One man wore thin glasses and his name was Lenscarry and the other had almost no hair and his name was Shadelost. Gina doubted she would remember who was who, but she would try.

Havemann was her prime concern.

After all introductions were made and the five of them were seated around the table, Havemann started off by asking a question before Gina could say a word.

"You said humans occupied millions of galaxies? How is that possible?"

Gina glanced at Benny and he nodded, clearly telling her she should go ahead and explain some history, something they hadn't done much of with The Creators.

"When your people left human space four million years ago," Gina said, "humanity was just starting to spread out from its home galaxy."

"Four million years?" Havemann asked, clearly stunned.

"Your people slept for the first million of those years of travel," Gina said. "Then what you called 'the great awakening' happened. But as we said before, you are a far distance from human-occupied space."

"During those millions of years," Benny said, "a group of long-lived humans spread out, seeding on habitable planets the basis of more human societies and helping them reach maturity."

"That's why we are called Seeders," Gina said. "Millions of galaxies are now alive with humanity because we seeded humanity on them."

Havemann nodded, then looked into Gina's eyes and asked simply, "Are we going to be able to rejoin the mass of humanity at any point in the future?"

"That's exactly why we are here," Gina said.

Beside her Benny was nodding.

Havemann sat up straight and glanced at the two men beside her, then back at Gina.

"We believe that you and your people have sacrificed enough in this fight," Gina said. "Our scouts have found a wonderful planet and system for your people and another system and planet for The Exterminators' people. Both in the same empty galaxy."

"How far away?" Havemann asked.

"At your speeds," Gina said, "about one hundred thousand years. But we can transport your entire fleets of ships in one of our mother ships and have you there within four years."

"Four years?" Havemann said.

Gina nodded. "In the direction of humanities area of known space."

"You can start fresh and build and eventually join all of humanity from there," Benny said.

"Why would you do this for us?" Havemann asked.

"It's what we do," Gina said, hoping Havemann would ask no more.

"We are Seeders," Benny said. "Our entire mission is to help humanity grow and flourish. We will be there to help you as well if you need it and ask for it.

Otherwise we will just stay out of your way and invisible."

"And we will protect the outsides of your galaxy from any chance the aliens will get there," Gina said. "But we require one promise in return."

Havemann nodded.

"We require that you will never try to build an alien race again in any fashion."

Havemann looked at Gina for a moment, then just broke out laughing in a high, light laugh.

Beside her the other two were laughing as well.

"That, Chairmen," Havemann said, "after the last few hundred thousand years, will be an easy promise to keep."

TWENTY-FIVE

BENNY AND GINA, over the next full year, worked with the humans on both fleets to toss away their bombs and start learning how to build homes and planet dwellings. Benny had no illusion that these two fleets of humans were in for the task of their lives.

And for many generations into the future.

What Benny was the most excited about was in that year, they got the two fleets to agree to work together to learn and build trade agreements between their two cultures. Everyone on all the ships would spend the four years in travel to their new home learning about living on the surface of a planet.

Benny had no doubt that a vast number of them would never be able to leave their ships. But a large percentage would, and that would be enough to start the two cultures.

So everyone on board the two fleets was going to get a crash course over four years while on the mother ship *Evening Tide* in living on a planet and building towns and eventually cities.

And maybe even how to make shoes. Not one person on either fleet wore shoes.

What had pleased Benny over the last year of working with the two fleets was the fact that Chairman Havemann and Chairman Airst of The Exterminator fleet got along great.

Both of them felt that this was a huge gift for their people.

Now, in just a short year, both fleets were docked on board the *Evening Tide*. In just a few hours, the *Evening Tide* would start the journey to take them to their new homes.

Benny found that amazing.

They were sitting across the same conference table in the *Stahl* with Chairman Havemann. The *Stahl* was docked on the large main deck of the *Evening Tide*, something that Chairman Havemann had found amazing.

This final meeting was to basically say goodbye. Benny had no doubt that he or Gina would ever see Havemann again. He liked her. She had courage and intelligence and the ability to think for all her people.

They had talked for a few minutes about the crash education program that was going to be offered in the next four years. Then Havemann looked up at Benny and then at Gina and sat forward.

"Can you tell me something in private?" Havemann asked, her expression suddenly very serious. "I promise to take your answer to my grave."

"That depends," Gina said. "Ask and we will tell you if we know the answer or can tell you or not and why."

Benny nodded.

"What is the real reason behind this sudden desire to help us find a home?" Havemann asked. "We all know the battle against the alien spread is not going well. Why do you want us out of the way? I understand we were not helping much, but we were helping, weren't we?"

Benny laughed and glanced at Gina who smiled.

"Yes, you were helping," Benny said.

Gina said into the air, "*Star Rain,* please ask *Evening Tide* for permission to put a privacy bubble around this room."

"Done," *Star Rain*'s voice came back clearly. "Your complete privacy is guaranteed."

"Thank *Evening Tide* for us," Gina said.

"I will," *Star Rain* said.

"Wow," Havemann said, shaking her head.

"Your fleets were helping overall," Gina said. "It was not a method that Seeders condoned or would ever do because we believe in letting a race make their own decisions on a planet."

"Which is why we are stopping their expansion outside of each galaxy," Benny said. "What the aliens do inside the galaxy is their business. We just can't let them expand anymore."

Havemann nodded. "And if stopped, they will die off because expansion is the only thing they know to stay alive."

"Exactly," Gina said.

"So if we were helping," Havemann said, "why pick this point to get us a new home and take us out of the fight my ancestors caused?"

Benny glanced at Gina and then turned back to Havemann. "Because we have better help arriving in a couple of years."

"Better help?" Havemann asked, clearly puzzled.

"At least five million ships to help stop the aliens," Gina said. "And they will all have the new, fast trans-tunnel drives as we do."

"Wow," Havemann said. "That will turn the tide."

"Eventually," Benny said. "Or at least we hope so."

"So who is bringing these ships?" Havemann asked.

"That's the part we can't tell you," Benny said. "Even under a promise of secrecy."

"But they have one requirement for joining the fight," Gina said.

"Let me guess," Havemann said, nodding. "No humans can know about who they are. So it was time to help us find a home."

"A win-win situation is how we looked at it," Benny said. "After millions of years, you finally get a home and out of a war."

"And we get help that might be able to stop the aliens," Gina said.

Benny watched the small chairman nod her head slowly.

"I have to be honest," Havemann said after a few moments, "I doubted we could hold our fleet together much more than a few more generations. So this timing is perfect. A complete win for us."

"Good," Gina said.

"In fact," Havemann said, "the truth is we were discussing asking for your help to pull us out of the fight before you arrived with your offer."

Benny laughed. "Great minds think alike."

"And you know we would have helped if you asked," Gina said.

"I know that now," Havemann said.

She stood and moved around to shake Benny and Gina's hand as they stood as well. "I have to get my people learning how to live on something that isn't metal and flying through space. Going to be a very quick four years."

Benny smiled at the chairman. "I have a hunch you'll get them ready just fine."

"I hope so," Havemann said. "And I hope this fight here goes as well as you plan."

"So do we," Gina said.

With that Benny and Gina transported back to the command center of *Star Rain*.

Two hours later, from their apartment, Benny and Gina watched as *Evening Tide* vanished, taking two amazing fleets of humans to their new homes.

Benny actually felt sad to see them go. And considering how angry he had been at them when they first arrived here all those years ago, that was pretty amazing.

And when he mentioned that to Gina, she just nodded, then said, "I felt like I have just said goodbye to a friend."

"We did," Benny said. "We did."

SECTION SIX
A Much, Much Bigger Problem

TWENTY-SIX

AFTER THE DEPARTURE of the two human fleets, it took almost five years for the first Gray ships to start arriving. It seemed that they had a few more problems with containing the alien outbreak than they had thought they would have.

Gina hadn't been the slightest bit surprised.

The other scout ships had found no other outbreaks, so now the daily routine had settled into battle reports and meetings with newly arriving chairmen to brief them on the problems they all faced.

The six chairmen had started having dinners together every other week to just informally talk about the problems and compare notes. They switched apartments for each dinner and who did the cooking and Gina had started looking forward to those nights.

They were wonderful breaks every few weeks with friends. There really were no notes to compare. The battle was still lost and with every passing day, the aliens spread out more and more, a flood that even though they were trying, there seemed to be no way to stop.

Every few months Benny would ask *Star Rain* to calculate the odds of victory against the aliens and every time, without fail, even with the Gray ships pouring into the area, the answer was zero percent.

Now, after ten years and over three million Gray ships and almost a million Seeder ships, that answer from *Star Rain* seemed wrong to Gina. To Gina, it seemed as if containment was starting to happen. But when Benny did his standard question, *Star Rain* said once again zero percent chance of defeating the aliens.

Benny and Gina had just finished going over the daily reports from not only their area of battle, but the other three major areas when Benny asked his question.

"That seems so wrong," Gina said.

Benny shrugged. It had been the same answer so many times, Gina doubted Benny even heard it anymore.

"We need to ask the question in a different fashion," Gina said.

Benny shrugged once again and indicated she should try.

"*Star Rain*," Gina said. "Will the area of battle that we focus on every day ever be contained?"

"Yes," *Star Rain* said.

Benny's head snapped up and he stared at Gina, a total look of shock on his face. She hadn't seen him be this surprised in a very long time.

And she felt exactly the same way.

She chose her words carefully for the next question.

"How long will complete alien containment of this area take?" Gina asked *Star Rain*.

"One hundred percent containment of this battle area will be achieved in approximately six-hundred-and-seven years."

Benny opened his mouth, but Gina stopped him from speaking.

"How long will containment take in the area *Star Mist* focuses on?" Gina asked.

"Fifty years less," *Star Rain* said.

"And the area *Star Fall* focuses on?" Benny asked.

"Approximately the same amount of time as this area," *Star Rain* said.

Benny stood there, his mouth opening and closing as he stared at Gina. Behind them the light chatter of the command center had silenced. Gina could tell that everyone was shocked by these answers.

"Let me ask the next question," Gina said to Benny and he indicated she should go ahead.

"So this entire battle area will be contained and the aliens defeated in this area in just over six hundred years?" Gina asked. "Correct?"

"That is correct," *Star Rain* said. "At the current levels of fighting and technology. More ships or other fighting advances will shorten that time frame by factors."

Benny just shook his head.

"*Star Rain*," Gina said. "When Benny has asked you repeatedly the chance of defeating the aliens, you have always responded with zero percent chance. Please explain."

"There are other alien incursions," *Star Rain* said.

Gina wanted to just sit down on the deck in front of her command chair. She felt sick.

Completely sick.

"You have got to be kidding me," Benny said.

"I am not joking," *Star Rain* said.

"How do you know this information?" Gina asked.

"I had access to the Creators' ancient records," *Star Rain* said, "many of which were not even accessed by those on the Creator ships."

"Oh, no," Benny said, turning and walking away a few steps.

"*Star Rain*," Gina said. "Please explain."

"The Creator's fleet continued movement for thousands and thousands of human generations. Much information was lost in those generations to the humans on board. The aliens were first created and planted just over two-point-one millions years ago and the human ships moved on without stopping to study their project."

"They forgot, didn't they?" Gina said.

"The information on the alien culture was stored and most likely forgotten, yes," *Star Rain* said. "The reason was that the alien growth would have taken dozens of human generations before the aliens would even have built their first ship."

"Ah, the standard impatience of humans," Benny said, shaking his head.

Star Rain went on. "The information and experiment was discovered again six-hundred-and-ten-thousand years later and the experiment was tried again."

"Let me guess," Benny said, "they did not stick around to see the results and it was forgotten again."

"That appears to be the case," *Star Rain* said. "The third experiment was attempted two-hundred-and-eighty-thousand years ago, leading to this outbreak. The human fleets did not move on this time and realized their mistake and attempted to stop the spread."

"But the first two attempts were never stopped," Gina said.

She just wanted to walk away from all of it. How was this even possible?

"I have no evidence to prove otherwise," *Star Rain* said.

Gina just shook her head. No wonder Benny's question always had the same answer. With two other outbreaks going for far, far longer. *Star Rain* was correct.

They really did have no hope.

Zero percent chance that humanity and Seeders and Grays could be saved.

TWENTY-SEVEN

BENNY TOOK a few deep breaths and then glanced at Gina. "We need to show this to the others."

Gina nodded. "And Ray and Tacita."

Benny nodded. "*Star Rain,* would you please ask the chairmen of *Star Mist* and *Star Fall* to join us here in the command center? Also invite Chairmen Ray and Tacita. Tell them it is an emergency."

"They have all agreed," *Star Fall* said after a moment.

Benny glanced back at their command crew, many who were looking very worried. "Everyone listen closely, but do not interrupt."

All the crew nodded as if their heads were pulled by the same cord.

A moment later Carrie and Matt appeared, looking worried. Right behind them Angie and Gage, also looking concerned.

"Been a while since an emergency meeting," Gage said.

"About ten years," Benny said, realizing he hadn't missed emergency meetings in the slightest.

"I'd have been happy with another ten," Matt said.

Benny could only agree to that.

"Bad?" Angie asked.

"Very bad," Gina said.

At that moment, Ray and Tacita showed up.

All of them were standing, facing each other in front of the command chair.

Without a word, Benny asked *Star Rain* his standard question that he had been asking for years.

"Zero percent chance," *Star Rain* said.

He noticed that around him everyone but Gina nodded. Clearly they all had been asking the same question of their ships.

"Now," Gina said, "let me ask that same question in a different way."

She asked about containment of their area and the entire area of the three command ships and *Star Rain* said six hundred plus years if there were no more advances in fighting technology. Less if more ships joined the battle or there were advances.

Benny could have heard a pin drop in the back of the massive command center.

Gage shook his head and spoke first. "The two responses do not make sense."

"They do if there are other alien incursions," Benny said. "*Star Rain,* please explain about the Creators' ships as you explained it to us."

After *Star Rain* finished, again intense silence filled the command center.

Ray and Tacita both looked washed out, as if they suddenly had no blood in their faces.

Carrie and Matt just stared at each other.

Angie and Gage looked angry.

Benny knew they needed more information to even get moving at all, so he said, "*Star Rain,* please show the path of the Creators' ships after their awakening to this area of space. Illustrate that path with a green line."

All of the chairmen turned toward the big screen as *Star Rain* first put up what looked like a mist-like three-dimensional cloud. Benny knew that each tiny dot of light represented a galaxy or group of galaxies. The scale was impossible to grasp in any real way.

A green line zigzagged through the mist. He knew it had taken The Creators almost three million years to follow that line.

Benny then said, "Please show with a red dot the first alien experiment location."

A red dot appeared back near the point of the start of the green line.

"At normal alien expansion," Benny said, "please show in red all affected galaxies from that experiment."

"This would assume the aliens of the first experiment were identical to the third," *Star Rain* said. "There is evidence in the records of the Creators that they were, but it is not definitive."

"We understand," Benny said. What he didn't want to say was that maybe the first aliens were even more efficient.

A vast part of the cloud turned red.

"*Star Rain,*" Ray said, "would it be possible to adjust the scale of this to also show in green the original human galaxy and the human-settled area of space?"

"Certainly," *Star Rain* said. The scale shifted to take in billions more galaxies and the original human galaxy blinked in green and all human galaxies were in green.

The red line and the green line looked impossibly close together. And the number of red galaxies far, far outnumbered the human ones.

"Oh, no," Tacita said softly.

"*Star Rain,* please estimate how close the aliens are to the human galaxies at standard trans-tunnel speed?" Benny asked, his stomach now twisted down into a tight lump.

"At closest possible incursion with these assumptions," *Star Rain* said, "Approximately eighty thousand years."

Silence.

Finally Benny said, "*Star Rain,* on this same illustration, pinpoint the second Creator experiment and the projected expansion of the aliens."

A second red cloud of galaxies filled the mist and actually overlapped the first. Thankfully that cloud went away from human space, but more than likely toward Gray space. Benny had a hunch they were not going to be happy to hear that.

Benny just stared at the vast wall of red. The area they were fighting right now, that would take them six hundred years to control, was just a small blemish on the larger area.

The scale was impossible.

"*Star Rain*," Ray said, "what is the likelihood that this scenario is a reality?"

"Sixty-one-point-two-three percent," *Star Rain* said.

Benny just shook his head. Way too high, but the only way to be sure was to go look.

And those alien areas were a long ways from where they were now.

A long ways from any Seeder ship, actually.

TWENTY-EIGHT

GINA STOOD THERE staring at the huge cloud of red and the small cloud of green. And the Gray controlled area wasn't even marked because no one knew exactly what the Gray area of space was.

But Gina did know the Grays were in this fight completely as well. They had hives on almost every human planet in every galaxy. If the humans were overrun, the Grays would be as well.

Silence around the eight of them filled the command center. It wasn't a good silence. And if the feeling of hopelessness she was feeling became the way of life, they would all be in trouble. Something had to be done and done soon.

"*Star Rain*," Gina said. "How long would it take this ship to get to the edge of that second expansion from here at full speed?"

"Ninety-one years," *Star Rain* said.

"And to the first expansion area?" Benny asked, following her lead.

"Two hundred and ten years, approximately," *Star Rain* said. "Again, using these assumptions."

"We need faster ships," Benny said.

Slight nods.

Benny turned to Ray and Tacita and waited until they both looked away from the image of red and were looking at him. Gina liked it when he did that. It got people, sometimes including her, to pay attention.

"The new drive we have, if my understanding is correct, is a standard trans-tunnel drive with seven other trans-tunnel corridors opened inside it."

"That is correct," Ray said.

"And each tunnel gives us another factor in speed, correct?" Benny asked.

Gina wasn't sure what Benny was asking, but he was pushing for something.

"Yes," Ray said. "It doubles with each new tunnel. Two, four, eight, sixteen, and so on."

"So we need faster ships," Benny said. "We have to go look at that area and find out exactly what is going on and we can't spend hundreds of years doing that before we act in response."

Benny waved at the big map of red and Ray and Tacita both nodded.

"So get those two who invented the new trans-tunnel drive working on more speed," Benny said. "We need to get there in twenty years, not two hundred. Faster if possible."

Again Ray and Tacita nodded.

"The six of us and our crews will spend the next three days running over every bit of data we can dig up from the ancient Creator records and every possible scenario," Gina said.

The other four chairmen were nodding, letting her and Benny take the lead.

"We need you to find out if even more speed is possible and if so, how long would it take to retrofit all three of our ships," Benny said.

"All three?" Tacita asked.

"You put us in charge of this fight here to win it," Benny said. "We are the young ones, remember, the ones who can face unknown situations and deal with them, as we have done here."

"This fight is now in control," Gina said. "You need our crews and our three ships fighting that situation."

She pointed to the big red mass of galaxies.

The other four chairmen were nodding, clearly in agreement.

"Meeting on *Star Mist* in three days?" Benny asked, looking directly at Ray. "Can you have the information about increasing speed by then? We're going to need it and a lot more if we're going to save not only humanity, but Seeders and the Grays."

"We'll have it," Ray said, nodding.

Tacita nodded as well.

Around them, Gina could feel the hopelessness slide away and the new focus starting to grow in their bridge crew and among the other chairmen.

"*Star Rain*," Benny said, "please remove that image. We all have work to do."

A moment later the cloud of red and green vanished and Ray and Tacita vanished with it.

"Meeting this time tomorrow?" Angie asked, glancing at the other chairmen.

Gina nodded, as did the rest of them.

And a moment later the other four were gone.

Benny reached over and took Gina's hand and smiled.

Then the two of them sat down in their command chair and went to work.

SECTION SEVEN
Finally, Some Good News

TWENTY-NINE

BENNY AND GINA hadn't slept that much over the last three days. They had spent a vast amount of time in their command chair, digging detail-by-detail through the records that *Star Rain* had retrieved from lost information in the Creators' ships. They had only moved for meals, showers, and a few hours of sleep.

It seems that *Star Rain* had been correct, the Creators had basically tried the same experiment three times in the almost three million years they had been in space. And they had tried no others, of any kind, thankfully.

But the more Benny and Gina dug, the more Benny was convinced that the aliens they had been fighting here were exactly the same as the ones created in the first two experiments. They were rats bred to build a basic space ship and expand into space. Nothing more.

And what Benny found headshaking was all the reasons for the three experiments. It seemed to always start when one some young scientist or historian dug up the reason they were in space. And that led to the discovery of the "experiment" as it was called.

All three times the pattern had been exactly the same.

And all three times the reasons had been forgotten when the ships moved on and the scientists doing the experiment died off.

The last day before the meeting with Ray and Tacita and the others, Benny and Gina had worked out how the front lines of the first two experiments might be expanding. It was a vast front, but they also had almost eighty thousand years before that front hit human-occupied galaxies. So they had time.

But on the scale that Seeders worked, that was almost no time at all.

Finally, they had *Star Rain* feed their conclusions to the other two ships and stood.

They were both very worried about the coming meeting. But they had a plan, one worked out with the other chairmen. But that plan assumed that Ray and Tacita would report with a possible chance of more speed.

Benny took Gina's hand. "Ready?"

She nodded and a moment later they had jumped to the familiar meeting room of *Star Mist.*

Angie and Gage were already there and seated, as were Carrie and Matt.

Benny considered the four chairmen he and Gina's best friends. The years had done that for them, and if the plan was implemented that they had worked out to fight this new battle, the six of them would be together for a very long time.

And that didn't bother Benny in the slightest.

Before anyone could say anything, Ray and Tacita appeared and took their chairs at the end of the large wooden table. Both were dressed as they always dressed, in black silk pants and shirt for Ray, and black silk pantsuit for Tacita.

Benny just watched as they got settled and then Ray looked at each of them for a moment, then said, "The inventors of the faster trans-tunnel drive believe they can increase the speed by three factors safely."

"Wow," Angie said.

Benny sat back, surprised because that was not the answer he had expected.

"For us math challenged," Matt said, "what does that actually mean for the two hundred year travel time to the first possible experiment location?"

Ray nodded. "The ten-year travel time from the local cluster which contains the Milky Way Galaxy to here would take seven months now. The two-hundred-year travel time would take just over two years."

"Wow, just wow," Angie said.

"That sounds great," Benny said, "But why am I expecting a large qualifier."

"Not a large one," Ray said. "They believe they can have the new drive developed and tested safely within ten years. They understand the theory, just never went beyond eight in the first building expansion because that was so much faster than before."

Benny nodded. He had expected that if the answer was positive on the speed issue, it would take time.

"We have already started the work," Ray said. "Scientists from all over known space are moving to help on the project."

"Star Mist," Angie said, "with the increased speed suggested by Chairman Ray, how much would that shorten the projected time of containment and victory in this area of this battle?"

"Containment would come within two hundred years if all ships were fitted with the new drive," *Star Mist* said. "Full victory would be within another two hundred years."

"Wow, good news for a change," Gage said, shaking his head.

Benny looked at Ray. "Honest assessment, please. Can the scientists do this?"

"Yes," Ray said without hesitation. "Possibly faster than ten years, but they asked for ten years to make sure the drives were completely safe."

Benny nodded, as did everyone around the table.

Safe was better. They were going to take enough chances as it was without having drive issues.

"Any idea if the conversion would be large?"

"The scientists don't think so," Ray said. "Adjustments mostly, from what they told me."

Benny was happy to hear that as well. That meant that all the small ships, the Sharks, could have the faster speeds quickly as well.

"So until then, we prepare and keep fighting here," Benny said.

"Push on getting this done," Gage said to Ray.

Ray and Tacita nodded.

"It might mean the difference between surviving and not surviving," Tacita said. "We understand that."

She and Ray stood and nodded, then vanished.

"Good news feels so damn strange," Angie said, laughing.

"Don't really know how to react," Carrie said, shaking her head.

Benny just nodded. It did feel strange.

But it wasn't for sure yet. And until they actually had ships moving at that promised speed, he would just wait and see.

THIRTY

FOR THE NEXT three years, Ray and Tacita reported monthly on the progress on the new drive. And each time to Gina it seemed promising. In fact, on the last report, the new drive had been tested and it had passed completely without problems.

So that was getting closer and seemingly ahead of schedule.

She and Benny had dropped back into regular routines and the dinners with the other chairmen had become planning sessions for the possible upcoming mission.

Part of the routine was for both of them to spend an hour every morning in the command chair, linked in with *Star Rain,* going over all the updates of the battle. It was during that routine that *Star Rain* informed them that Angie and Gage were asking for them in a meeting on *Star Mist* with Chairman West.

"Tell them we will be right there," Gina said.

They both stood, still holding hands.

"Is it possible after almost twenty years that West has some news for us?" Benny asked.

Gina laughed and shook her head. "Don't get your hopes up."

"Killjoy," Benny said.

"That's not what you said last night," she said, winking at him.

Benny almost blushed and a couple of the command crew behind them chuckled.

A moment later they were standing in the meeting room on *Star Mist.* Angie and Gage were already seated, as were Carrie and Matt. Ray and Tacita had just arrived and were taking their chairs and Chairman West sat next to them, smiling.

Gina could tell this wasn't a bad news meeting as she and Benny sat down. The mood in the air was light.

"Go ahead," Chairman West," Angie said.

West's smile got larger, if that was possible.

"We have recently completed final testing on creating large empty-space bubbles and keeping them stable."

"How large?" Gage asked a moment before Gina could.

"Stability can be maintained at just under two hundred light year diameter," West said.

Gina and Benny both sat back with that. They had been hoping twenty years before, when Benny came up with the idea, of managing just twenty or thirty light year diameter, and a hundred seemed like dreaming.

"Wonderful!" Ray said, smiling.

Gina was shocked that even Tacita was smiling at the news. Gina couldn't remember the last time Tacita had smiled. It looked almost wrong, actually.

"We also have figured out a way," West said, "to create an empty-space bubble that will be in motion. Only sub-light speed, but still in motion."

All of them congratulated West, then Benny asked, "So is the testing done? Can we try this on the battlefield?"

West smiled. "That's the next step."

"What is needed?" Gage asked.

"To create a stable bubble of two hundred light years in diameter," West said, "we need to explode enough of the empty-space bubbles within a reasonable distance of the new bubble at the same time. Too many and the new bubble is too big."

"How many smaller bubbles would that be, approximately?" Gina asked.

"A couple thousand," West said. "Easily done with the Shark ships."

Gina nodded. West was right. It would be an easy operation to coordinate.

"So when do you want to build this first one?" Benny asked.

Everyone waited for West to answer.

Gina expected the answer to be in six months or a year. After twenty years of West working on this, that seemed like a logical time frame to her.

"Tomorrow," West said. "That would be perfect."

All Gina could do was just stare at Chairman West's smiling face.

Beside her Benny just laughed with the other chairmen.

Good news was a very, very strange thing to get at times.

THIRTY-ONE

FOR THE FIRST test, they had decided on a corridor of alien ships that were pouring from one smaller galaxy and heading toward another larger one.

Most of the alien ships had not reached the new galaxy, but there were millions of alien ships on the way. And all seemed to be moving along a fairly narrow path.

The chairmen had decided that they were going to try to defend that galaxy and so far were succeeding against the early alien ships. But they had little hope of stopping over a million ships per day.

But an empty-space bubble would certainly help a lot.

Benny couldn't believe his crazy idea might actually work. He had basically given up on it after twenty years. And over the last three years his focus had been on the upcoming mission.

So this news felt almost surreal and he was in a complete wait-and-see mode.

Actually, everyone but Chairman West was. And after scanning through West's last few experiments that had been successful, Benny could see why West was excited and positive.

How they had solved the problem of constructing empty-space bubbles was to discover what drew an empty-space bubble to a certain location. They had copied that and then, when a bubble was deflated somewhere nearby, the replacement bubble formed where they had wanted it to form.

Benny and Gina had been standing in front of their command chair, watching the movement of the ships on the big screen of the area around the proposed empty-space bubble.

"*Rescue One* in position," *Star Rain* said.

Benny and Gina had decided to keep *Star Rain* back away from the test area. But *Rescue One* was close, a little closer than Benny would have liked, actually. But he had decided he wasn't going to second-guess West in any fashion.

"Anchor functioning," West said. "All systems green."

The Anchor was the device that would draw the empty space to it when one was deflated nearby. The Anchor was positioned directly in the center of the path of the mass of ships pouring from the nearby galaxy.

Gina turned to their command crew. "Stay alert on this one. I want data from every possible source."

Then she and Benny sat down in their command chair and Benny said to *Star Rain,* "Be prepared to move us to safety if anything threatens this area."

"Understood," *Star Rain* said.

Gina squeezed his hand.

"Chairmen, we are ready," West said.

Benny knew that all six of them were watching, as well as Ray and Tacita. But it was up to him and Gina to give the go-

ahead, since this experiment was in their area.

"Do all systems look clear, *Star Rain?"* Benny asked.

"All systems are ready," *Star Rain* said.

"It's a go," Benny said.

He still wasn't believing that after almost twenty years, his crazy idea was being tested.

"Stand ready," West said to the thousand Shark ships near empty-space bubbles.

They waited. Gina squeezed his hand as they watched the image of a thousand Seeder ships in empty space along with almost a thousand white dots indicating existing empty-space bubbles. All other ships and Gray ships had been sent out of the area for the experiment.

"Anchor working at full capacity," West said. "Bubble One Experiment is a go."

Benny knew at that moment *Rescue One* would coordinate all the destruction of the other empty-space bubbles. That had to be done basically simultaneously to make it work.

For a moment it seemed as if the experiment was failing until suddenly the screen showed all of the empty-space bubbles vanishing at the same moment.

And then, a moment later, a large, large area of the screen showed a perfect sphere, shining white.

Benny knew he was holding his breath because this was the key moment. Would the huge empty-space bubble stabilize?

"How large is that?" Gina asked *Star Rain.*

Two hundred and seven light years in diameter," *Star Rain* said.

"Too much?" Benny asked.

"Too early to tell," Gina said.

One of the worries was how to measure the amount of empty space in all the other bubbles and how that would fill in volume this one large bubble. Clearly they had missed by a little in that calculation.

"The new bubble seems to be stable," *Star Rain* said. "The next sixty seconds will be important."

Nothing was coming from Chairman West yet.

Benny tried to force himself to breathe normally.

Rescue One was still in position and Benny could only imagine the intensity they were working on board that ship. This had been a passion for the crew of that ship for twenty years.

The seconds ticked past and Benny and Gina kept getting more and more data flowing in.

But neither one of them, or any of the other chairmen wanted to interrupt the work on *Rescue One* to ask a question.

Benny found being a spectator difficult at best. But with his hand in Gina's, they sat there, trying to breathe and focusing on the data.

Finally, after almost two full minutes, Chairman West said simply to all of them. "The bubble is stable."

"Confirmed," *Star Rain* said.

"Unbelievable," Benny said, standing.

Gina stood and hugged him harder than he remembered being hugged before.

Behind them, the entire command crew was cheering.

After so many years, they all so needed positive news.

And setting up a vast trap for alien ships was about as positive as it got.

Benny just couldn't believe his wild-hair idea had worked.

And he had a hunch his face was going to be sore from the grin, since grins had been few and far between before now.

THIRTY-TWO

OVER THE NEXT five hours, more and more amazing data poured into *Star Rain* about the first test experiment.

So much that at times Gina couldn't seem to keep up.

The best that could be determined from the wreckage of alien ships in the small empty-space bubbles that were popped, over six thousand alien ships had been destroyed almost instantly. One of the bubbles had had almost two hundred alien ships in it.

And Chairman West had been correct that by suddenly deflating an empty-space bubble, anything inside was completely destroyed.

After five hours, she and Benny took a break for a late lunch or early dinner. Gina couldn't decide what to call it, and then went back to their command chair.

They managed to get about five hours of sleep that night before a meeting on *Star Mist* with Chairman West and the others.

When they arrived, Gina thought it felt just flat wrong. Everyone was smiling, including Tacita.

They had had so many serious meetings in this room, fun seemed out of place.

But everyone was laughing and joking.

Gina found it infectious, mostly because she felt exactly the same way.

West looked like he hadn't slept at all and Gina doubted he had, but his mood was jubilant, to say the least.

So for the first thirty minutes of the meeting, he gave a solid report on the successes and a few minor problems they had discovered that could be fixed easily.

"And no repercussions when we pop an empty-space bubble this size?" Angie asked.

West shook his head. "A thousand others will form shortly after, but that would be it. Gravity and time forces will just rebalance. Or we could have another nearby Anchor and it would form another large bubble."

"Are we going to test that?" Matt asked.

"We will, yes," West said.

Finally, it was Gage who asked the question both Gina and Benny had talked about last night and both were curious about.

"How fast can we put these large bubbles out there?" Gage asked.

"That will be up to all of you," West said, smiling. "It will totally depend on how many ships you would like to divert to the process."

"Are you saying that is the only limiting factor?" Ray asked, leaning forward.

Gina was surprised by that as well.

West nodded. "The Anchors can be easily mass-produced and a bubble formed in less than two hours of work. So each bubble needs a coordinating ship and as many Sharks as needed to pop enough smaller empty-space bubbles to make the desired size of the larger empty-space bubble."

"It took your ship and about a thousand Sharks yesterday, correct?" Angie asked.

West nodded.

Gina had a hunch they were going to be doing a lot of calculating very soon on how to disperse fleets of ships to this task.

"How close together can these large bubbles be?" Benny asked.

"Safely," West said, "eight-hundred light years apart. We have not tested that, of course, but the math tells us that is the answer."

Gina just glanced at Benny who was shaking his head. She felt the same way. In the distances between galaxies, that was extremely close together.

"So we could put these up around an alien galaxy, basically," Gina said, looking back at West. "On all the major paths alien ships take toward another galaxy?"

West nodded. "Let me show you, if you don't mind if *Star Mist* downloads a few images from *Rescue One*."

"Please," Angie said.

"Star Mist," West said, "would you please show the first image I prepared from *Rescue One* of the path of the alien ships from the origin galaxy to the target where we put the large bubble yesterday?"

"I would be glad to," *Star Mist* said.

A moment later an image of two galaxies appeared in the air, one near Ray and Tacita and one near Angie and Gage.

A white sphere floated between them directly in the path of a mass of tiny red dots that were alien ships.

"This second image is a very rough illustration of how the alien ships leave one galaxy toward another," West said.

Gina watched as a cone appeared. At one end it was basically the shape of the origin galaxy and expanding out like a megaphone toward the larger target galaxy.

Gina was amazed. All alien ships already in transit were inside the cone and the large white empty space was square in the middle of the cone and about halfway between the two galaxies.

Now Available
from all your favorite booksellers
in trade paper and electronic editions.

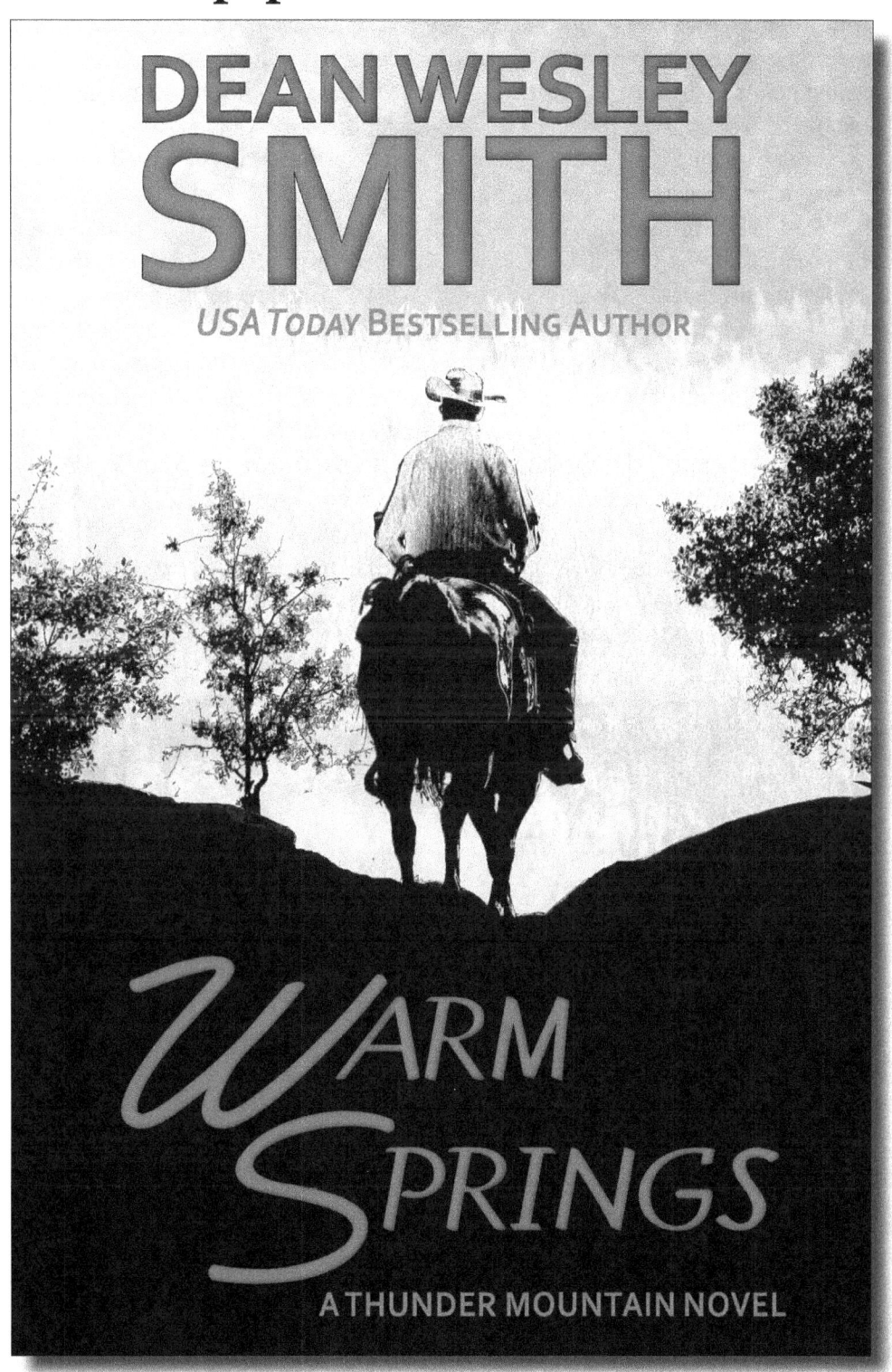

"Here is what would be needed and would be possible to stop most alien ships in that corridor," West said.

The image changed to show six large white empty-space bubbles staggered behind the first one and offset in such a way that almost no alien ship could escape hitting one of them.

"A couple dozen Sharks could clean up the few ships that make it along the seams," West said, smiling.

The stunned silence filled the room. Gina could hardly breathe. Was this even possible?

Ray and Tacita just sat there, eyes wide, staring at the illustration floating in the air.

Finally Matt asked, "How long did you say it would take to set that all up?"

"Using the fleet we used yesterday," West said, "two days at most."

Again Gina just sat there beside Benny, stunned. She didn't even know what to say.

Two days?

Just two days?

Nothing in the world of Seeders took only two days.

"Star Mist," Angie asked, breaking the silence, "how many alien ships, approximately, will leave that galaxy along that corridor?"

"Approximately sixty-four million," *Star Mist* said.

"Let me see if I understand this completely," Ray said, turning to face West. "You are telling me we can stop sixty-four million alien ships with two days work and a dozen or so Sharks watching for those alien ships that miss the bubbles?"

"That's exactly what I am saying," West said, beaming.

Silence.

Then everyone in the room jumped to their feet applauded.

West looked embarrassed, but kept his grin pasted on his face.

Now Available
from all your favorite booksellers
in trade paper and electronic editions.

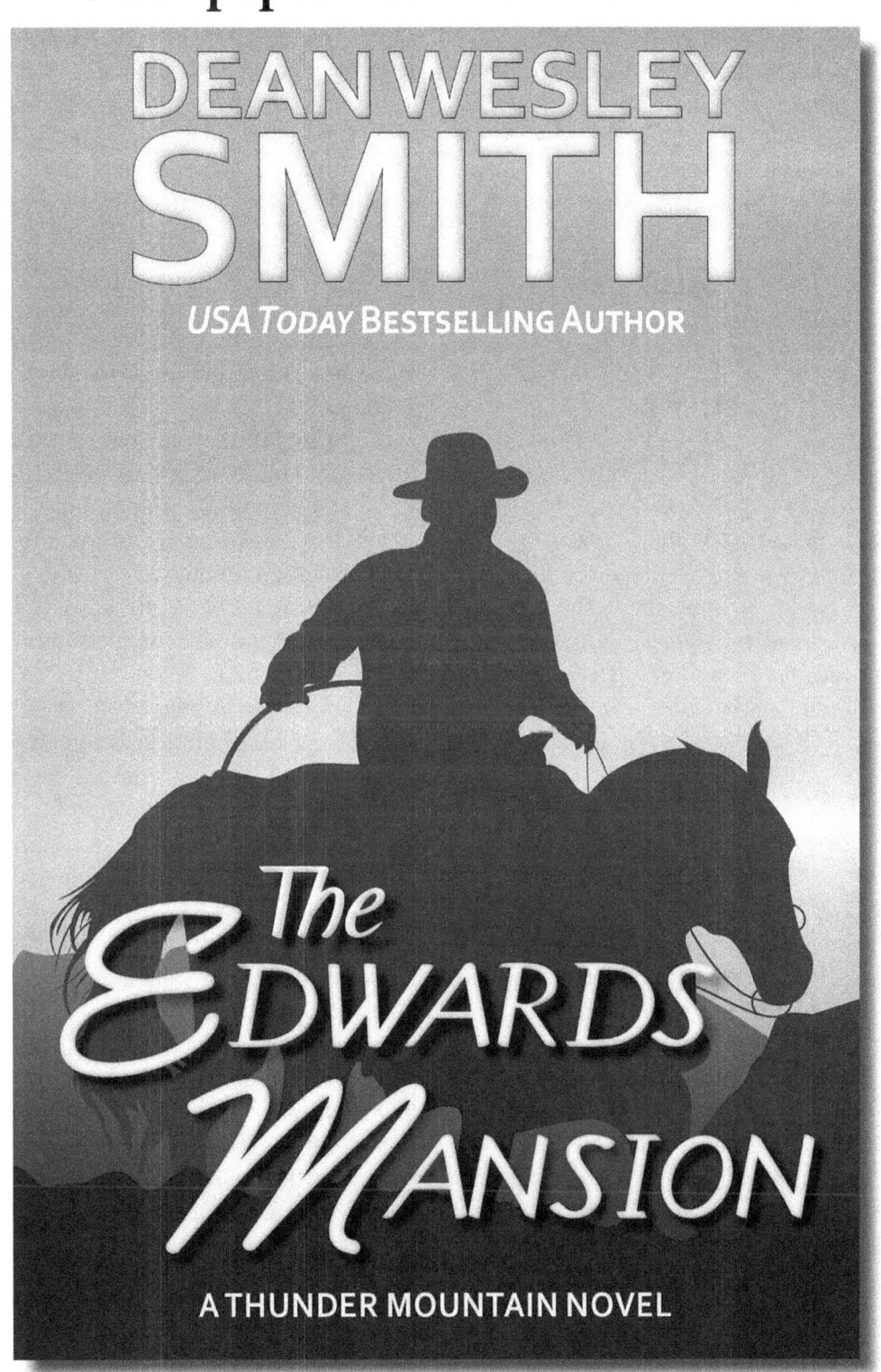

Gina couldn't remember feeling this good before, at least not since they had found the alien problem.

Beside Gina, Benny applauded while he shook his head and then laughed.

"What are you laughing about?" Gina asked him.

"It's going to get real crowded in those rattraps," he said.

She liked the sound of that more than she wanted to admit.

THIRTY-THREE

BENNY AND GINA stood in front of their command chair, watching the daily reports pour over the large screen in front of them. Around them, the mood in the command center was light and there was occasional laughter.

In the weeks after the first initial successful construction of a large empty-space bubble, Benny and Gina and the others worked with West to form teams to build new bubbles.

Or rattraps as Benny liked to think of them.

Larger military ships that could hold a thousand Sharks were the anchor ships.

And by the end of three weeks, they had ten fleets of ships placing bubbles.

Ray and Tacita had managed to get the Grays to join in the guard duty of any alien ship missing a bubble. It seemed the Grays were very impressed at the Seeders' ability to come up with solutions and were more than willing to help.

By the end of six months, most of the Seeders' fleets were involved with building bubbles and the Gray fleets were doing cleanup around the bubbles.

As a test, West and his team had built a large bubble right in the middle of a large number of alien ships, then waited a few weeks and popped it to make sure the result would be as desired.

Benny was happy to learn that the result was better than hoped for. Deflating a large bubble smashed whatever was inside into pieces so small, they were hard to even identify. Basically, everything inside became nothing more than space dust.

And when the test bubble was deflated, a new large bubble formed close by with another Anchor.

So now, at the one-year anniversary after the first bubble had been formed, hundreds of thousands more rattraps were formed, with Seeder fleets creating them at the rate of six hundred per day.

Benny just shook his head when he learned that number. Seeders never did anything at a small scale.

And tonight, on the one-year anniversary of the first bubble, all the chairmen and command crews from all the major ships in this fight were meeting for a large party to honor Chairman West and his fantastic team. The first real party they had had out here.

Benny couldn't believe how much he was looking forward to the party, and Gina had spent days trying on different dresses, she was that excited as well.

And she had made him promise that he would dance with her no matter how many left feet he claimed to have.

They had earned a party as far as Benny was concerned. They had done the impossible and won this battle.

It would still take years to block all main alien ship corridors, but only years. Not decades or centuries.

And that just made Benny smile. He still wasn't used to thinking in the vast numbers of years that Seeders thought in. He liked here and now and maybe some thought of tomorrow. So this schedule worked for him.

He just wasn't good at thinking about next century.

But now, officially, this battle was won. *Star Rain* had estimated at this rate of construction, the entire alien problem would be contained in ten years and the aliens would cease to exist in this area of space in less than two hundred years.

It would take longer in the larger areas of infection, but not that much. Not now.

And when he asked *Star Rain* the percentage of chance of this entire battle being won, the answer was now one-hundred-percent.

That was worth a party by anyone's rights.

Gina came over and took his hand and smiled at him. "Ready to go get dressed?"

"I am dressed," he said, smiling at her.

"I mean in the tux I got for you," she said. "I'm dressing up and so are you."

"How many decades have we been together?" he asked. "You ever seen me in a tux?"

"That's going to change tonight," she said, kissing him. "And I'm looking forward to it."

He laughed. She knew he didn't really mind. But he had to pretend to complain.

She took his hand and then turned him so they could face the command crew that had backed them so well for so long.

"Everyone," she said, "time to go get dressed for the party."

"Star Rain," Benny said. "Take care of things until we get back."

"I will," *Star Rain* said. "Enjoy your party. You have earned it."

"We have all earned it," Benny said. "And that includes you."

"Thank you," *Star Rain* said after an uncharacteristically long pause. "The honor has been all mine."

#1... October 2013

#2... November 2013

#3... December 2013

#4... January 2014

#5... February 2014

#6... March 2014

#7... April 2014

#8... May 2014

#9... June 2014

#10... July 2014

#11... August 2014

#12...September 2014

#13...October 2014

#14...November 2014

#15...December 2014

#16...January 2015

#17...February 2015

#18...March 2015

Now Available
from all your favorite booksellers in trade paper and electronic editions.

USA TODAY BESTSELLING AUTHOR

DEAN WESLEY SMITH

HEAVEN PAINTED

as a Free Meal

A GHOST OF A CHANCE NOVEL

Thank You!!

I would like to thank the following wonderful people who support my blog and my work through Patreon. Your support is very important to me. Thanks!

Irette Y. Patterson

Chris Cousino

Jane Lawson

Shantnu Tiwari

Rob Cornell

Erick Lindman

Christopher Ridge

Miguel Angel Alonso Pulido

Nancy Hendrickson

Ryan M. Williams

Jacob Proffitt

Marian Goldeen

Brenda Bergeron

John Connelly

Gary Speer

Megan Bryce

Michelle Tatam

Ann Tucker

Kari Wolfe

Terry Mixon

James Husun

Kathryn Rooney

Sherman Cox

Chong Go

Maria Grace

Grondpom

Fen

Livia Quinn

Amri Ackers

Robin Brande

J.R. Murdock

Kathleen McClure

Michael Kelberer

Gunnar Gunderson

F.I. Goldhaber

Mary Jo Rabe

John Kilgallon

Dave Hendrickson

www.ingramcontent.com/pod-product-compliance
Lightning Source LLC
Chambersburg PA
CBHW081151170626
46813CB00009B/3156